MW00424399

Dedicated to Dad, our packmates,
and my fellow canine warriors.

SENIOR CHIEF TURBO

MEMOIR OF A NAVY SEAL K-9

Based on true events

By R. C. Cook

Coyote Hill Press

Published by Coyote Hill Press, Riverside, California

Layout & Design by Robin S. Hanks

First Edition, 2013

Printed in the United States

ISBN: 978-0-9912641-0-0 All rights reserved.

Preface

A wooden door swings open and three men shuffle out onto the dirt road, their hands raised above their heads. The pack is lined up next to the wall of an adobe compound that is still radiating warmth from the day's sun. We are on high alert, watching our opponents' every move. I look for signs of aggression as they pass by me, but the shadows hide their faces. Their fluttery pants brush my nose; I smell fear on their skin. I am back in Afghanistan.

My packmates tie up the three men. Nerves twitch in my legs – I can smell more opponents inside. Dad's fingers release my leash and I sprint under an arched doorway and into the courtyard, catching whiffs of burnt earth as I scan for human scent. In the first room, I leap over folded blankets and across the floor mats. Finding nothing, I dash out, making passage through a teammate's legs.

The smell of roasted lamb lures me into the next room where I find an abandoned leg of mutton hanging on an iron bar over a mound of ash. I chomp down, tugging at the elastic skin and licking charred fat off my lips. I swallow three enormous bites before the nagging thoughts of Dad convince me to move on.

I run back out to the courtyard and sniff the air.

Something is different... Wrong. My ears perk, my head swivels, but there is no sound. Now I am alone inside the adobe walls. I sprint to the door, and out onto the dirt road where our footprints are etched in the dust. *Did they leave?* My pulse thumps in my ears; my stomach cramps. I need to find my Dad.

I take a few steps down the road where I'm surrounded by the steady hum of crickets – their pulsating scream drowns out everything else. I turn and walk back up the road, stopping again to check the compound. It is empty; even the rooms I just searched have disappeared. I run further – the road leads me up to a cave that seems to rise out of the ground as I approach. I sniff the area for hints of Dad.

Then a long rumble erupts from deep underground, and in the pause that follows, I detect radio tones. The game is on.

I hear the echo of Dad's voice, and I dive head first into the darkness, slamming right into a bony set of legs and taking a knee to the chest. As my eyes adjust to the darkness I see goats – hundreds of them. They fill the cave, moving toward me with a slow, mindless resolve. I charge ahead, hoping to part the herd down the middle – but they panic – dancing nervously and threatening to stomp on my paws.

A couple of the goats stiffen as they try to get out of my

reach. I already know what is going to happen next – I watch them teeter along on unbending legs, paralysis spreading into their backs; and they sway, top-heavy, before finally falling hard to the ground. The hysteria reverberates through the crowd, and the entire goat infantry starts to faint, one row tipping over onto the next.

I climb the goat pile, leaping over their backs as they crash to the floor. Bombs shake the ground, and the bodies under me wobble. Dust rains down from the ceiling. The pile seems to grow higher with every step, and the air is thick with their stench. My hips are aching, but I need to find my Dad. *I must get to him.*

A burst of air rises out of the cavern's depths. It rushes over me like cold water, washing the goat smell from my nose and fur. Another scent passes by – peppermint and blood – and my heart pounds. *He's hurt!* I gallop over the berm of goats. My legs are numb; it feels like I'm flying. I bark to him – *I'm coming!* My ears fold back. *I will find him, no matter what.*

Then I hear a crunch of sand, a short stride approaching. My eyes pop open and lock onto the kid shuffling towards me.

"Hooyah Senior Chief Turbo."

I watch the kid vault onto the platform that is shading my nap spot. He scrambles around on the boards overhead.

Another student runs up a minute later, as the first slides down a rope behind me. "Hooyah, Senior Chief," the second kid says before leaping up out of sight.

My muscles start to relax. It's a warm day in Coronado, and waves are crashing on the beach. There are no booms or blood or goats. These kids don't know about our deployment games yet, but they will soon enough – and we are training them to be champions.

I fill my lungs with ocean air and then exhale out a groan while my legs stretch. I see Dad in the distance, holding his coffee mug and talking to the other instructors. Then I find a cool patch of sand where I can plop down and doze off again... the BUD/S students and seagulls following me into my dreams.

Chapter 1

Holland

I came into the world on a rainy morning in Holland, greeted by a beautiful blonde Belgian Malinois with glowing amber eyes. I was the first in the litter to arrive, covered in a wet, dark coat of brindled fur. A sister who followed me out was nearly solid black – very little stripe – but my next two sisters to emerge were golden like my mother. My brother appeared last, shivering, tiny and pale. I don't remember much of those first hours, but we spent the next few days sleeping in a warm pile of tummies and fighting for a feeding spot under my mom.

As our litter grew stronger, we began to explore the pen. We sniffed old pees and crumbs of kibble, and sometimes found a bug to harass. When there was nothing new to discover, we pounced, wrestled, and tail-whipped each other to the point of exhaustion. Then we collapsed into the hay for a nap until a new ambush was launched, and it was time to play again.

My mother hovered nearby, always watching. She kept us safe, herding us back from the pen's edge when we collected there to peek at the world beyond. And her jaws kept us in line when the games turned rough. The day I learned how to flip my sister using her enormous ears, my mother immediately responded with a sharp pinch on my neck. I yowled, pouting for a bit... then I nuzzled my mother's face and begged her forgiveness. After that, I only needed a sideways glance from her to adjust my behavior.

Just as I started to learn the rhythm of family life, I was taken away. A brown-haired man appeared one afternoon with a small boy in tow. The man's rough hand sorted through our bin, gripping the back of my neck and lifting me high in the air where he examined my undercarriage. With a quick descent my feet were back on the ground, and the man and his son disappeared – we listened as they visited dogs in neighboring pens.

"Well, which one do you want?" we heard the man say in Dutch.

Little feet shuffled towards us. The boy reappeared at the edge of our bin and pointed at me, and the man scooped me up. I hung in the air for several moments before I was dropped into the boy's waiting hands.

"Okay," he said. "We'll take this one. And you will help with his training." The boy's head nodded.

The boy carried me to their car and lowered me into a

box, and we drove towards smells of water. I whined and whimpered; I missed the pen filled with hay, my siblings. The scent of my mother was slipping away – thinner and thinner – and then it was gone.

The boy opened the box lid and stroked my head a few times.

"Remember, he is not a pet," the man said, pronouncing the words with sharp "z" sounds. "He will be a working dog, maybe a champion, and we are his masters. Don't get too attached."

The boy's hand slid out of the box and the lid closed.

"You picked the best one," the man – Master – said in a softer voice. "His father was a champion."

The boy remained silent, but the box trembled from him nodding.

The car slowed to a stop, and I caught glimpses of grass and wispy trees through the box's portholes. Fresh air rushed in as we left the car and the box bounced in unison with the boy's steps, Master's scent close behind. We made our way down a hill towards a line of concrete kennels.

"Put him in the last kennel, next to Bastien."

The box set down and tipped over, and I rolled out

onto the hard, frozen floor. The other residents yapped greetings from their kennels as I wiggled to my feet and wandered around the empty space, sniffing streaks on the floor as my pads went numb. There was no hay. No mother and no milk. Nothing.

I whimpered, the sound repeating like a hiccup until it formed into one fluid howl, but I opened my eyes to find that the audience was gone. Master and his boy were already hiking down through the thick wet grass towards the farmhouse. There was an outburst of barking – a reminder of an upcoming mealtime – and then my neighbors fell quiet, and Master disappeared behind a door.

A few hours of silence confirmed there would be no more visits that evening, so I settled in. It was my first night alone in the world. The only light came from the glowing orange farmhouse windows – I could smell hints of food in the smoke puffing out of the chimney. I wrapped myself into the tightest ball I could and stared out at a sea of grass beyond the bars until my lids fell closed.

I awoke the next morning with a starving belly and a full bladder. After a stretch, I peed on the corner wall of my kennel. Relieved, I performed a tumbling routine and then sat down to scan the farm for signs of life – there was a line of ants in the dirt fronting my cage, and rabbits near the barn munching on an unlimited grass buffet. The birds were my favorite, hopping and chatting; they scattered into the sky when Master approached with our kibble.

Master shoved bowls of food into the other kennels, but he stopped short in front of mine. I turned in circles and begged for my meal, but he propped my bowl on a high wall and opened the door, grabbing the scruff of my neck. In a blur of motion, I spun around to view my own pee stain as Master whipped my butt and bellowed, "*Fooey!*" In another blur, he lifted me out of my cell and dropped me onto the grass.

"You go here!" He pointed his finger.

Shocked at the quickness of it all, I wandered through the tufts and sniffed a brown spot that smelled like the other dogs. I peed on top of theirs.

Master leaned down, giving me two long strokes down my spine. "Yaah, *braffy*," he whispered. "That's a good boy."

He returned me to my kennel where the food awaited, and I ate while the neighbor dogs heckled. "*Master does not like to clean kennels!*" they warned.

After morning kibble, Master released us in turns. Klaus, a muscular 2-year-old with a thick brown coat, was first out. Master unhooked the kennel door and Klaus made a beeline to my cage, pissing on the front bars and drowning the troop of ants. He snorted like a bear and lumbered off, leaving behind a heady stench.

When Klaus returned from the field it was Bastien's turn for recess. He emerged from his kennel – a young, honey-colored dog – tail wagging and ready to play. As he passed, Bastien pressed his flank into the wires of my kennel, letting me get a good sniff. He gave me a lick, like a friendly nod, before trotting off with Master.

I was next up for release. Master attached a leash to my collar and we hurried out to a great open field, past clucking chickens and a goat that lived on the riverbank. Master stopped in the short grass and took out a rope toy that jerked to life in his hand. I caught it in my teeth and we pulled back and forth, the strings flossing down into my gums. Every time Master tugged I imagined it was one of the chickens, and my legs sprung to rip it from his hands. I loved the challenge, and the feeling of energy in my jaws. It was playtime.

When I clamped down with my back molars, Master would give me extra praise, "Yaaah, *br-r-r-raffy*! Good hound!" He rolled his r's with a smile and patted me on the head.

When Master grew tired of tug, he reached into his pocket and pulled out what would become my greatest obsession – a ball. The ball is perfectly mouth-sized.

It can be caught, held, and chewed – but it can also fly, like a bird without feathers. My legs trembled as Master's arm coiled back and he threw it into the sky. I sprinted down the field under its shadow, like a racecar moving through gears to get to top speed. The ball hit the ground, and an uneven bit of earth bent its path, but I swung right to snatch it and sprinted back to Master for another throw. Every time it left his hand I tried to beat it to its destination, sometimes just to punch it back up into the air with my nose.

"You have a high hunt drive," Master announced, more to himself than me. We walked slowly back to the kennel while I panted to catch my breath. "You will make a good scent dog and bring in a high price."

In the days that followed, Master and I practiced his games, and I worked to memorize his words, studying the twitches of his face and mouth. *Zit!* meant he wanted my butt on the ground – the sharpness of the "z" wrinkled his nose. *Bliven* was the command to stay – his lips parted before his top teeth bit his lower lip. When he wanted me to walk on his left side, he told me to *fooligan*. His lips would pucker out as his brow gathered in the center. The correct response won me the ball; the wrong one resulted in a jerk of the leash and a *fooey* – the Dutch word for no.

A lot of Master's words were just a jumble of sounds – I understood the tone but not the meaning, which didn't

help me win games. I preferred his hand signals –
Master's palm lifting to his shoulder for a sit, pushing
towards the floor for a "lie down," or thrust in my face
for a stay. They were direct and easy to understand.

When we completed the day's games Master would
give me a few minutes of freedom, and I used it to
run. I ran so far and fast, the air rushing past my belly
seemed to lift me off the ground. Sometimes the boy
would join me on the field, and we would chase each
other through the thick pastures. The boy would stop
and creep toward me, and I'd crouch down, lowering
my ears. We would lock eyes, and then I'd launch right
at him. His muscles tightened as I ran by, missing him
by a hair and making him giggle. Even Master would
laugh as I tore down the field like my tail was on fire,
covered in dew and gasping for air.

Walking back to my kennel, Master said, "I've never
seen a puppy love to run so much. He runs faster than
Klaus even! We will name this one Turbo."

I bounded over to my cage. Klaus, who had overheard
Master's boast, barked to remind all of us who the
alpha dog was. The next morning, he drove the point
home in the form of a stinking pile outside my kennel.

****

Weeks passed, and my new quarters grew more

comfortable. We had plenty of food and daily recesses to play. In addition to training with Master, the boy gave me extra free time, which made Klaus crazy. He constantly threatened to fight me; but we were never released together, so I ignored his tantrums. I was consumed with my next recess, when I could feel the earth on my pads and try to steal a taste of last night's dinner from the garbage dump. I was always on the lookout for snacks, often nibbling goat turds during practice.

Master and I started using a rough jute bar for our tug games. It was a stick that smelled like hay – its weave made for a nice, tough chew. Master would reveal the bar from behind his back and hold it out while hissing the word "*stellan!*" Before he could finish the word I leapt, latching on with my feet off the ground, body twisting in the air.

I tugged at the bar until it stopped squirming, and Master commanded me to "*los!*" with pursed lips. The first time he gave me the "*los*" command, Master became very still – and I hung on the bar until my jaw ached. When I finally dropped in surrender, the bar sprang back to life. Then Master's ragged teeth peeked out as his lips parted with a smile – followed by another "*stellan!*" – and I jumped to catch the bar in my mouth. After a few more trials, I learned that the quicker I let go after a "*los,*" the faster play resumed.

Once I had a strong record of bar game victories, we practiced a new event – tug with an actual human arm. The first time Master's assistant slipped on a jute sleeve and Master whispered "*stellan,*" I just stared at them, searching their faces for information. Master's eyes were intent, and he repeated "*stellan*" so emphatically that I launched and bit just above the wrist. The assistant struggled, and we pulled back and forth in a battle for the sleeve, the weave slipping around in my front teeth.

I looked at Master for support, and he came up behind and pressed the back of my head forward. I took a deeper bite of the sleeve and felt the arm beneath.

Master stroked my head. "Yaah, braaff, good hound." His face was proud.

Over the course of our practices Master taught me to bite with a full mouth, crushing the sleeve in my molars, my lips stretched tight. Once I understood the technique, Master declared me the winner of every match. Sometimes I even won the sleeve, which I carried it around in my own victory parade.

Eventually my opponents graduated to wearing thick fabric bodysuits; I knew the *stellan* game was about to start when a padded man took his position at the end of a clearing. Master would hiss the command – *stellan* – and I'd sprint towards my opponent, jumping to bite the arm or armpit. Once attached, we tussled until he surrendered. Whether the match was long and laborious or over quickly, I was always the winner.

One dark and cloudy afternoon we drove to a new training site – a field so long I never did find its end. The van creaked to a stop and the engine rattled before going silent. I searched the cold air in the window cracks for familiar scents, *traces of my mother?* But the only odors I found were hints of grass and countless men and dogs. Still, my feet pranced in hopes of a long run, chasing a ball.

Master got out of the car and the door banged shut behind him. I whined, begging for release, but he walked off towards a bunch of men and never looked back. I sat in my kennel for hours, tormented by the scent of a ball hiding in the front seat.

The click of the hatchback jolted me awake, and cool air rushed inside. Master attached the leash and I leapt from the car, straining against my collar – I wanted to sniff every blade of grass, identify every dog that had run here before me, but Master tugged me along behind him. We walked up to a group of men with white hair, like patches of snow on their heads. Vapors of grain liquor swirled around us in the icy breeze.

After some discussion about past champions, most of the men collected at the sidelines to watch our first game. Master surprised me when he pulled a metal-toothed chain out from his pocket – I moved quickly in reverse at the sight of it.

"Eh! *Fooey!*" He said, his face serious.

I froze as he clamped the heavy collar around my neck and attached it to my leash. The prongs made my skin itch.

Master pulled a rope tug from his corduroy pocket and tossed it towards an assistant's waiting hands. My eyes were locked on it, but the weight of the neck prongs kept me seated.

Master walked me over to a short hurdle. The assistant flaunted my rope tug on the other side – it was just dangling from his hand. We stepped up to the bar.

"*Hoog!*"

Master's face was intense, but I didn't know the word. I began to walk around the hurdle, but he gave me a yank. The prongs nipped my neck.

"*Fooey! Hoog.*"

I looked at Master's eyes for clues. Finding none, I went to climb over the bar – but as soon as my paw touched it the collar bit me on the neck.

"Fooey! Hoog."

Two more *"fooeys"* later, Master demanded I *"hoog"* again – this time I jumped over the hurdle, trying to reach my toy in a single leap.

"Yaahh *br-r-raffy,*" he whispered, his smile spreading into his eyes.

I tugged the rope away from our assistant, and Master gave me a proud thump on the chest. The white-haired men buzzed about me being a "fast learner."

"He's going to earn me twice as much as Klaus," Master announced. Klaus had disappeared a week earlier.

We practiced the *hoog* command several more times, using taller and taller hurdles. Then we practiced *fooligan* – walking at Master's side – and *bliven,* which required me to sit very still while he walked away. After several good showings, Master returned me to the car with a pat on the head and a "good braff." I drank water and rested, waiting for my next turn.

Master began driving me out to that field every afternoon to train for "KNPV" – the Dutch police dog trials. After Bastien and a new pup returned from their morning recess, Master and I drove past the long rows of crops out to the KNPV field. I stayed behind in the car while Master wrapped a heavy coat around his shoulders to venture out into the drizzle; I listened to his footsteps as he walked away, the mud sucking at his rubber boots. I waited and enjoyed the warmth of the car – the more time that passed, the more likely Master would have whiskey on his breath when he returned. It was a good smell – it made him easier to please.

We practiced our games in front of the white-haired men and a few curious rabbits – events that included jumping over ditches, climbing walls, and attacking opponents as they rode a bike. He demanded my full attention during competition; even when a gun was being fired during the event, or when there were other dogs off leash nearby, he was angry if I got distracted.

Master also began teaching me the "zook" game – finding hidden objects that had been thrown into the woods. It was mostly pipes, sometimes coins, and once a ball so big I had to roll it back with my nose. Each time, I turned the item into Master for the most excellent reward: a tennis ball. The zook game quickly grew on me – I started frisking Master for the rubbery smell of tennis balls at every release.

But the white-hairs' favorite game was stellan, and I was their star attraction. I enjoyed being downwind of my challenger, smelling his breakfast, and then soaring through the air to land my bite on the target. Whenever I competed in this event, the white-hairs chattered:

"He is a champion."

"Magnificent to watch."

"Beauty in motion," they said.

Master would try to hide his grin as they murmured to each other on the bench. He returned me to the car, my lungs burning and legs still twitching with adrenaline. But as the light faded in the windows, I relaxed into sleep, listening to the sounds of Master and the white-hairs howling in the whiskey barn.

****

KNPV training taught us how to protect our handlers from predatory humans – the kind who yell and stomp their feet, or threaten others with swinging sticks. We had been practicing bite work for over a year now, and I was in top form. The game was fairly predictable – I bit, my opponent fell, I jerked, he smacked and kicked, I thrashed around, and he gave up. I always won.

It was a chilly day in November when one of my opponents threw me a curve that changed the course of my career. I hopped down out of the car for our late afternoon *stellan* practice. My takeoffs and landings were legend among the white-hairs, who had gathered under the row of trees for today's game. We walked over to the starting line, blood rushing through my muscles at the sight of the puffy-suited man at the other end of the field. I sniffed the air, but his breaths rose quickly into the sky, taking their scents with them.

I fidgeted, waiting for the hiss of Master's "*stellan*." My opponent waved his staff, signaling readiness for battle, and I focused on his armpit where I would land my strike.

The "*stellan*" command came and my legs exploded into a sprint. I reached full speed and leapt at the shoulder, hitting him hard with an open mouth – but instead of falling away from the force of my bite, my opponent stood firm, with his weight pushed forward. I slammed into him – like hitting an oak tree – and heard a loud snap. A blink in time later I was lying on the ground, unable to move my head. I felt like an ax had been driven into my neck.

The white-haired men gathered around me; one bent down and pressed his fingers into my neck and back. I watched them huddle, squabbling with their coffee-scented mouths. Then Master ran up, growling and barking at my opponent.

"You idiot, you don't know what you are doing! Do you have any idea what this dog is worth? Do you realize what you've cost me? He could have been a champion stud!" His tone was guttural and his forehead was scrunched down around his eyes. Spit flew out of his mouth.

16

After an evaluation by one of the white-hairs, Master lifted me in his arms and carried me to the car. His chest heaved as he walked, and I listened to the voices behind us.

"That decoy was green."

"Shouldn't have been catching these dogs."

"He jammed Turbo up. Might have broken his neck," they whispered.

My opponent and I both left the field that day in shame, never to cross paths again. I spent weeks in my cage, barely able to move, my eyes fixed on the farmhouse below. When Master brought me my food, I could see the disappointment in his face.

A few days later, the boy started delivering my meals. He would hang out with me while I ate, stroking my head until his mother signaled him to return. I begged him to bring me a ball, but he refused.

"You need to heal. You're hurt," he said.

I was afraid I would never feel the chew of a ball again. I was a fallen star, no longer a competitor.

Months passed, and I slowly recovered. I could lift my head and trot through the grass with minimal pain – pain that disappeared altogether if there was a ball in play. But my relationship with Master had changed. When I was ready to resume training, a new handler showed up to drive me to the KNPV training field – a large man named Wally, who smelled like clogged guts. Wally knew all the commands, but we didn't enjoy playing the games together – we were both second-tier competitors, damaged goods.

I was wary of the bite game now. The event started as they always had – Wally said *"stellan"* and I ran towards a suited man down field. But just before the hit, I slowed to check my opponent for signs of a trick. My strikes had become overly cautious – and I was giving myself room to swing to the side if necessary.

The white-hairs agreed that I was no longer the champion I had once been.

"He used to take off earlier, *before* the injury."

"He used to hit harder. *That's* the difference. He's more tentative now."

"Turbo *used* to be beauty in motion," they said.

I was two years old when I performed at the official KNPV trials – Wally walked me through a series of events that lasted all day. He directed me to attack humans who rode bikes, and sent me to find objects hidden in the deep grass. I swam across a ravine to retrieve a wooden bar and then back to the shore again, my neck aching to keep my head above water. I jumped over and crawled under every kind of obstacle; I searched for and guarded humans and their possessions. Master and the boy watched me from the sidelines, their faces pleased.

When the tournament was over, I had passed all of the tests except for one – walking past a plate of food on the ground. I smelled the cooked chicken half a field away, but waited until it was within striking distance to pounce. Wally yanked me back with a stern "*fooey,*" but not before I got a taste. I lost some points for that event, and Wally was marked down for his sloppiness as a handler, but I still received the highest score in the competition that day. My picture was posted on the wall of the whiskey barn for all to see.

Chapter 2

The Americans

I knew the Americans were coming because the white-hairs were nearly feverish over the news. In between events they slurred about numbers and all of the things those numbers could buy.

We practiced everything that morning: obedience, bite work, and searching for humans in the woods. Our games were routine to me now – I could predict their rhythm and score quickly – but this week was special.

Master was in attendance, and he was cheering me on. It was like the days before my injury.

The boy was the only one unhappy about the Americans' visit. His face was sad when he visited my kennel; he pulled treats out of his pockets, and carefully wrapped his arms around my neck as I inhaled them.

"I'm going to miss you, Teer-bo," he said softly in Dutch. My tail wagged.

It was morning when I heard the leather boots crunching snail shells down the path to my kennel. The wind picked up and I caught a whiff of the oils from their skin. Four men rounded the corner and came into view; their bellies parted their overcoats, hanging over hefty belt buckles. I sat and watched as they collected in front of my cage, their eyes scanning me from various angles.

Master asked if they were police or military, and they shook their heads no.

"We buy dogs and train them for the military," one of them said.

"We sell to special operations mainly," another one growled. Master nodded.

The Americans' deep voices reminded me of Klaus,

with his habit of pissing on my cage front. They grumbled, brows gathering in the center, and their faces registered disappointment.

"He is a different dog out of the kennel," Master said, his tone calm.

Clipped to the leash, Master walked me to the part of the field where the ravine curved like a snake; the resident goat scowled at me and ran off. An American with big ears took a plastic pipe out of his coat and flung it deep into the high grass. I didn't see where it fell – Master was turning me in circles like I was chasing my tail.

My legs jack-hammered in anticipation. Master finally unclipped the leash.

"*Zook!*"

I ran, zig-zagging through the grass, hunting for the American's scent. My nose caught a faint smell on a westerly breeze and I ran, sliding through the marsh until I located the source. I emerged from the marsh with the pipe in my mouth – muddy, smiling, and ready for my reward.

The Americans nodded as Master directed me to "*los.*" I dropped it at his feet, wagging my tail as I scanned hands for more objects to be thrown. We played a few more rounds with a copper pipe that rubbed on my teeth, and then we played the last game with a fuzzy yellow tennis ball – Master had to yank my collar twice to convince me to let that one go.

Master's attention turned to our audience. The Americans were using their high-pitched voices.

"He *is* fast!"

"He has a hell of a hunt drive."

"He loves that tennis ball," they said.

Master took me to my kennel for a rest, and when I returned I saw one of the Americans – a young man with crooked teeth – cramming himself into a red fabric suit, and the rest of the Americans gathered at a wooden table near their padded friend. My legs trembled with excitement as Master walked me to the opposite end of the field. After what felt like an eternity, he thumped me on the chest and whispered, "*stellan.*"

I tore down the course, birds fleeing in my wake; then I launched. I could smell pig on my opponent's breath as I clamped down on his bicep. He wiggled inside of the suit, hitting me with his other arm and throwing me to the ground. I was surprised by his strength, but I came back at him with more intensity. We thrashed around for many minutes before he became still and Master gave me a stern, "*los.*"

I hung by my teeth for several heartbeats, daring the pig-scented boy to assault me again, before I finally dropped to the ground. Master clipped on my leash; and I kept an eye on my opponent, ready for his next move, my ears alert for a command.

The Americans' voices became so high they could only whisper.

"Bad ass."

"He did not want to let go."

"That dog brings the fight."

In celebration of my victory, Master pulled a ball from his pocket and threw it across the field. I chased it down and returned it to his waiting palm, slippery with spit. After the fourth throw he let me keep it, and I chewed and listened to the buzz from the Americans.

"He has no quit in him."

"That dog loves the ball."

"He'll make a good detection dog," they said.

The talk turned to numbers; then Master and I walked back to the kennel, both of our chests full with pride.

"Yaah, *br-r-raffy*. That's a good hound," he repeated,

patting my head.

The next day I heard the van pulling up to the property again. I smelled the Americans approaching – they were surrounded by an aura of bitter, hoppy gas.

My pig-scented opponent from the previous day's events coaxed me into a plastic kennel, which he lifted into the back of the van. I joined two other dogs, both frantically asking, "*Where are we going? What's going on?*" I didn't have any answers.

I had not received breakfast that morning – my stomach was growling with hunger. I searched for Master to remind him of my feeding time, but he and the boy were nowhere to be found.

The Americans closed the car's doors and we drove south through areas of Holland I had never seen. The structures grew taller with every mile, and they seemed to stare down at us with hundreds of glass windows. The cars around us drove faster and faster over the slick pavement, and our van raced to keep up with the stampede.

We arrived at a concrete field, where the smell of fuel stung my nose. The other dogs whined, "*Where are we going? Can I get out now?*" while the Americans mingled with other humans, passing around bags and papers. Finally, our kennels were lifted onto a cart that drove

us up to a huge, bloodless machine, and we were
loaded into its belly.

I listened to beeps and rumbles as I sniffed the bags
around us. I knew that my life was about to change
again. The other dogs barked, begging for a way out –
but the men heaving baggage into our compartment
were deaf to our whines. I searched for anything
edible, and then I gave up and lay down. A few
moments later, one of my travel companions released
his guts and filled our compartment with a beefy
stench.

The plane doors were sealed, and we enjoyed a few
moments of quiet before the engine screamed so loud
that my ears collapsed. The machine came to life,
rolling forward – slowly at first, then faster with a swell
of noise – and suddenly we were moving upward with
great force. The pressure hurt my ears, and a wave of
icy air flooded our compartment. Shivering, I tried to
sleep through the pain while the other dogs sobbed
and sat in their own waste.

Ten hours later, the machine hit the ground with a
clatter, limping to a standstill. The hatch opened and
bags around us were tugged out. I watched, my guts
aching from a full bladder and an empty stomach.
When all of the bags around us had disappeared, our
kennels were yanked off the plane and lowered to the
ground. We waited there, helpless, sniffing the ocean

air and rubber.

Finally, the pig-scented American and his friend met us on the tarmac and let us out of our cages. We raced around wildly, pulling against our leashes and tripping over each other at pee hubs, all the while scavenging for anything edible. We guzzled water from dirty puddles glossed with jet fuel. I hurried to complete my business before I was yanked back into my kennel, and we were loaded up for the next miserable leg of the trip.

Four hours later, we landed again. Our kennels were transferred to a warm van, and we endured another long ride while our noses defrosted. It had been a full day since we'd eaten, and I was sniffing for any signs of an upcoming meal. The other dogs had lost all hope, starving silently in their filthy cages.

We arrived at a farm with tall, swaying grass; the air smelled like corn stalks and sweet tobacco spit. I could hear the hum of wind funneling between barns, and dogs yapping in the distance. We were released from the car to stretch our legs as the Americans sprayed each of us with a water hose. After a few minutes of exploring, the guards guided us towards the first of three long, parallel buildings – inside, the din of a hundred dogs welcomed us with greetings and confrontations.

Entering through the wide metal doors, the pig-scented boy walked me past the taunts of my fellow prisoners.

"I'm going to kick your ass rookie!"

"Bring that butt over here."

"Look at me! I dare you!"

The rants echoed off the floors and rafters. I listened to the slip of paws on the floor, the sound of pacing in tight laps.

The pig-scented boy prodded me into a filthy kennel, and pushed a bowl of kibble through a hole in the door. I inhaled it and sniffed the floor for scraps, but all I found was old urine stains.

After several hours without recess, my stomach began to cramp from the new food. I looked for a human to let me out, but my neighbors warned me not to expect many visits. The afternoon was warm, and the air trapped in the building was heavy with waste; many of the dogs were wearing poop, or had painted it on their walls. But Master had trained me that messing your cage was the worst kind of crime. I would hold out as long as I could.

****

Days of imprisonment passed. I had one recess in the morning, when I was allowed to roam the hard patches of pee-soaked grass just outside the kennel house on a leash. A rusted barrel lying on its side was the favorite hub; everyone took turns adding their scent.

Middays were spent in lockup – I napped while others barked and paced. At night we received a large helping of kibble, most of it served on the floor, spilling out as the guard shoved the bowl through the door slot. For a few minutes after mealtime, a calm settled in to the kennel house, with the contentment of full bellies. But as the room grew darker, a few whimpers would steadily build into a series of barks, which would finally explode into a full-blown riot – the choruses waxed and waned until just before dawn. I slept as much as I could to escape the chaos, dreaming of grass fields and the lawn-mowing goat.

For the next two weeks, I wondered why the Americans had brought me here if we were not going to play any games; but one day word passed through the kennels that the "King" had arrived, causing a mild uproar. Legends of his temper spread from cell to cell, setting off the nervous spinners.

King was the supreme leader of the Americans – this according to my neighbor Rocko, a 55-pound Belgian Malinois who spent most of his day searching the back wall of his kennel for a hidden escape hatch. *"They are going to kill us,"* he repeated incessantly as he paced back and forth.

Then King appeared, strolling down the hall, radiating a hearty odor of tobacco and grease. He was a burly half-lion, half-man, with a head full of coarse gray fur. Some dogs stood in salute as he passed; others covered their gas leaks with their tails.

King led his human pack down the hall. Two of them were tall and lanky; three others – two men and a woman – were heavier and slower. They were all dwarfed by the King.

They paused a few kennels down from mine to view a dog named "Elvis." King announced that he was one of their "top eighteen" dogs, and the pack nodded, some of them leaning in to get a better look while the female scribbled on a clipboard. Then they continued their march down the hall towards my kennel, and I heard King grumble my name. I sat and watched them slowly bunch up in front of my cage.

"This one is Turbo. The team picked him up in Holland. He's one of the eighteen that we're going to show the special operations guys next week," King said.

The woman flipped papers and wrapped them around her clipboard. "Top scores on his KNPV. Good tracking and attack skills. Very high hunt drive. Fast."

A dark-haired man they called Rob hunkered down, his eyes squinting. "You sure he has what it takes? He doesn't look very confident."

The woman looked at the clipboard. "Carl gave him high marks for aggression. He wrote that Turbo is a 'different dog out of the kennel.'"

The other pack members grunted their approval of Carl, but Rob's eyes remained fixed on me. "We'll see," he said with a snort.

As he was rising to stand, Rob rattled the door of my cage – a meaningless challenge in light of the chain links separating us. I didn't move. I pictured him dressed in a bite suit at the end of a long grassy field, reeking of fear and cigarettes – I wanted to hear him squeak. But for now, stuck in a cage, all I could do was hope.

The fate of the "eighteen" dogs was the talk of the kennel house; the best athletes had been chosen, but no one knew for what. I suspected we would be competing in a tournament, but my neighbor Rocko was sure the humans saw the healthy dogs as a threat to be eliminated. He spent the morning murmuring nonsense about explosions, every so often barking, *"They are going to kill you! We have to escape!"*

Bruce, a thick German Shepherd across the hall,

believed the "eighteen" would be trained into a great dog army. He complained about not being chosen and threatened to fight me for my position, convinced that the Americans had made a mistake.

The next day, one of King's assistants came to my kennel, leash in hand – a tall man with shiny dark hair. He had been at our evaluation the day before, standing quietly behind the King, but now he spoke in a cheery voice.

"Hey Turbo, I'm Sam. Let's see what you can do!"

Sam released me from the kennel and, after a long pee, we trotted out to a grass field where he slipped a chain over my head. The cool wind carried smells of manure and rain – I begged for a sprint, but Sam clipped the leash to the chain and pulled out the slack.

"Let's do some obedience first. *Sit!*" He pronounced it with a soft "s" instead of Master's sharp "z," and yanked my chain as he said it.

My butt hit the ground, but I had already received a penalty choke – a sharp pinch on the neck. Panicked and confused, I looked up at Sam for help.

"Good boy," he said, his face relaxed. "*Plots!*" he yelled as he yanked hard on my leash.

I shifted my butt over to his side and straightened my

posture, staring up at his right hand for a tennis ball, as I had done a hundred times before. Sam looked down at me and wrenched my neck with the chain.

"*Plots!*" he ordered again, with another choke – but I was already performing the *plots* command, sitting at his left side. I stared up at his blank face.

"*Plots!*" Sam demanded more loudly, jerking my collar in frustration. I got up and ran a circle around him, making my way back to his left side where I sat again.

"No, dipshit. *Plots.*" This time Sam leaned over and yanked my collar towards the ground, collecting my skin in the ring. I kneeled, wishing Sam would put on a fabric suit so we could better communicate.

After several awkward rounds, Sam's face began to register a problem. He looked over at a truck parked nearby and yelled, "Hey Billy, what's the word for lie down?"

My pig-scented travelling companion appeared from behind the truck. His eyes looked into the sky for a moment, and then he yelled back. "Is that Turbo?"

Sam nodded.

"He's Dutch so it's *off*."

Sam leaned over and shouted, "*Off!*" as he tugged the

chain towards the ground, his tangy breath blasting me in the face.

The word sounded close enough to *"auf"* that I lay down on the wet grass, the bugs wiggling to escape from under my belly. I wished I could explain to Sam that our problem was not one of volume.

"Good boy," he exclaimed.

We practiced heeling and jumping over hurdles, both of which I figured out by context. Each time Sam gave a command he yanked my neck – then when I performed, he flattered me with praise. It was a puzzling rhythm, and it threw me off my game.

At one point Sam commanded me to stay in one place, mumbling *"bly"* with his palm in my face. As he walked away, I thought about escaping – just running at top speed and disappearing into the distance. I knew by the spare tire around Sam's waist that he wouldn't be able to catch me.

But then Sam yelled *"here!"* and I ran back to him, without enthusiasm.

Sam attached my leash and we trotted over to the truck. "He's okay on obedience," Sam said. "Let's do some bite work."

The pig-scented boy nodded and stuffed himself into

a fabric suit, and we moved into dueling positions at the far ends of the field. He clapped his hands, inviting my charge, but I knew from the smell of anxiety on the breeze that he remembered me from Holland. My legs vibrated as I felt Sam's hand touch the clip attached to my collar.

"What's the command?" Sam yelled.

Don't worry about it Sam, I thought. *I've got this one.*

Sam yelled something as he unclipped my leash and I ran, slowing for a split second before I launched, my jaws open wide. The pig boy fell sideways when I hit. I wriggled my teeth through the fabric, feeling for muscle underneath.

"Whoa! Okay, yep, he can still bite!" he cried.

We wrestled. I could smell his distress, like sour cheese. He shifted around under the suit's cushion, his face covered in sweat. I was dominating the fight.

I heard Sam's boots clomp up behind me, and I listened for a "*los*" – but instead he pulled hard on the chain around my neck, closing off my throat. I wanted to yelp at the pain, but I couldn't make a sound, stumbling as he pulled me backward.

When he finally released his grip I gasped for air. I turned to look at his face for signs of anger, rage, or disappointment, but Sam just patted me on the head.

"Good dog," he said with a maddening grin.

We walked back to the kennel house and Sam ushered me into my cage. Rocko was eager to hear news of my day, but I didn't know how to explain the practice. I told him that we had played a game I couldn't win.

Rocko yapped at me, turning in quick circles. *"Have they tried to kill you yet?"*

I didn't know. *Maybe, once or twice…?*

Rocko was sure that all of the top eighteen dogs would be executed. He returned to searching the back of his kennel and scratching at the floor, all the while grunting, *"We gotta find a way out of here… we need to escape."*

Chapter 3
Meeting My Dad

The florescent lights of the kennel house blinked on one morning before the sun rose. When word passed that King had made an appearance, the residents went berserk. Some dogs flagged their tails, others tucked. My neighbor Rocko curled up like a pill bug, trying to disappear. *"They're coming for you,"* he warned.

King strutted down the main hall, leading a large pack of humans. Some of them were eager, revolving around King's booming voice; others wandered more. One – a loner – hung back behind the crowd, scanning the kennels with a critical brow.

The group made its way down the hall, finally arriving at my cell. "And this one is Turbo, another dog we'll be taking a look at," King said.

I remained seated while the group gathered, evaluating me with varying levels of interest. Then the loner appeared and took center stage, kneeling down in front of me; he had blue eyes and smelled like peppermint. *"Who are you?"* his face seemed to ask as he looked me square in the eye.

"He doesn't look like much in there, but he's one of our top prospects," King said. "He will definitely make it into one of your programs."

King turned and clomped down the hall, leading the group to the next "eighteen" dog. The loner stood slowly and began to follow, his eyes flashing back at me.

The group cleared out of the building, and soon after, Sam began taking the "eighteen" dogs out to the field one by one. Each of them trotted out, ears and tail erect, ready to put on a show. When it was my turn, Sam entered the kennel house and unlatched my door.

"Come on boy, let's show 'em what you can do," he said

as he clipped on my leash. He was much more excited than I was.

We passed through the parted metal doors, and my eyes adjusted to the bright sun. A swarm of twenty or more men of all shapes and sizes were waiting outside. They gave off clues about their status – some took up space with wide stances, a few had fidgety hands; others were defensive, arms folded over soft middles. The blue-eyed loner was very still, his arms at his sides, a paper cup in one hand.

Sam and I faced our audience while one of King's assistants shuffled through the tall grass behind us, hiding something for me to find. Sam turned around and commanded me to "track" into the dusty field – I took off, moving over crushed leaves and following traces of odor that were ripe in the day's heat. My nose led me to a plastic pipe that I snatched, rushing back to exchange it for a tennis ball. I enjoyed five glorious chews of my reward before Sam choked me and I spit it out.

We played several "track" games before I returned to the shade and incessant chatter of the kennel house. Sam locked my door and walked off towards the next competitor's kennel as I lay down on the concrete for a nap.

Across the hall, German Shepherd Bruce was still

proclaiming his rightful place on the "eighteen" roster. *"It's not fair – I am stronger than all of you!"* he growled. My neck ached as I listened to his tantrum. I would have happily given him my place with Sam.

Rocko was whining next door. *"The electrocutions are coming,"* he warned.

A few hours later, Sam began retrieving each of the eighteen dogs again, leading them down the hall for a bite event. After several dogs returned, tails wagging in victory, Sam came to escort me from my kennel. We walked out to the field, and as we passed the humans I overheard their chatter.

"Elvis is a prettier dog."

"I want to see what Turbo can do – he looks mean."

"I think he's too quiet to be a good attack dog," one whispered.

"Turbo is one of our best bite dogs," King declared. "He brings the fight, no fear."

My opponent waddled out in a thick fabric suit, and I walked to the opposite end of the course on tingling legs. Sam mumbled a word close to *"stellan"* and I felt the leash give way. My feet pounded the dirt in long strides, my lungs pumping – I aimed and leapt, landing on the decoy's padded collarbone and hooking my lower jaw into his armpit. The man inside squealed as he fell backwards, writhing under the suit, but I pinched down as he tried to slip out from beneath my hold. He banged my side with a stick and kicked me in the thigh; I fought harder. With a secure grip, I rolled and thrashed to twist his skin between my teeth.

Sam cheered. "Yeah, Turbo! Get him!" But seconds later, he crept up to choke me from behind – I felt his hand on my collar, the jingle of a chain, and I let go as it tightened on my neck. Sam hurried to attach the leash, and the humans crowded around me.

"He has great intensity."

"It's between him and Elvis – they are the top two."

"He seems kind of cold. Like he doesn't give a shit."

Then the blue-eyed man approached, and once again we exchanged curious looks. He lifted my chin and rubbed his palm down my back. "I like his demeanor," he said, crouching next to me. "He's calm – less hyper than Elvis."

The blue-eyed man stood, and Sam guided me away to the kennel house. I looked back at him a couple of times, until we turned the corner.

Back in lock-up, Rocko pressed me for information. When I told him I had won my match he was not

41

pleased; he urged me to stop revealing my skills to the enemy. Rocko returned to digging at the concrete floor as I settled in, tuning out the barks that echoed down the hall. That night I dreamt of Holland – the hush of nature, smells of the water, and the boy, with pockets full of treats.

The next morning I woke up sick in my stomach. I tried hard to ignore it – to sleep – but the ache nagged. Next door, Rocko spun in circles, repeating his usual chant, "*They are going to kill you. We have to escape.*"

As the morning progressed with no sign of Sam, I finally gave into the pain and fouled the corner of my kennel. Toxic waste sputtered out of me, filling the cage with stink. As I broke Master's most sacred rule to the tune of Rocko's paranoid song, I wished escape were an option.

It was early afternoon when Sam finally appeared to let me out; and as he clipped on my leash, his face screwed up at the smell. We passed Elvis on our way out of the building, being led by one of the other trainers, and the two of us exchanged sniffs. "*Have fun!*" he chirped as he walked down the hall to his kennel, his golden tail wagging.

Sam and I ran over to the buildings where we practiced a game he called *sook*. It was a little different than the "*zook*" game Master had taught me, where I sniffed out toys he flung into the marsh. In Sam's version of *sook*, certain odors made a ball magically appear from the wall – like the sweet smells of cherries, almonds, or rotting fruit, and the sour odors of eggs, menthol, ammonia, or bleach. I would learn later that these were the scents of our opponents' bombs.

The first time we played *sook* a few weeks earlier, Sam seemed to be making up the rules as we went. He commanded me to "*sook,*" but then he dragged me around the room on leash, pointing out the different smells. When I sniffed them he yelled, "*sit,*" and then choked me before my butt could hit the floor. A ball popped out of the wall; I chewed it for a minute until he choked it out of my mouth.

At first I thought there was no way to avoid the repeated assaults in Sam's bizarre game, but after a couple more rounds he let me play one by myself – he ordered me to "*sook!*" and I searched the walls and cabinets while he stood and watched from a safe distance. When I found an area that smelled like ammonia, I sat, and a ball popped out of a hole in the wall; I scrambled to catch it and enjoy a good chew. When Sam started to approach, I dropped the ball before he could strangle me and we ran to the next room, where I sat next to some bleach odor and another ball was revealed. We played this version of *sook* several times each day, and it quickly became my favorite – an easy game with minimal choking, the ultimate reward, and very little Sam.

Entering the *sook* buildings for our exhibition that day,
I scanned the audience, which was divided into two
groups – a small huddle in the front row with their eyes
focused on Sam and me; and all the rest gathered in
the back of the room, coffee mugs in hand, paying us
little mind. The men up front were quiet, intent – and
one of them was the loner with the blue eyes.

Sam attached my long leash and told me to "*sook*" a
large, cluttered room. I darted behind stacks of boxes
and sprang up to sniff countertops until I honed in
on a cupboard trapping the smell of rotten fruit – my
butt hit the floor and a ball appeared from a hole in
the wall. I snatched it for a couple of chews and then
spit it out when Sam started towards me. We played
throughout the building, and every time I sat, a ball
appeared.

When I had located all of the scents, Sam let me
keep my final ball reward as the men in the front row
crowded around me again. King stood to address
them.

"I think everyone agrees that Turbo and Elvis are our
top two dogs, so it's just a matter of which one you
guys want to select. SEALs have first choice this time,
Army SF gets second," he said.

The man with the blue eyes came and sat beside me, and we had a soundless conversation. We were the loners – the dissenters – and we were fearless. He rose and said, "We are going to pick Turbo. I like his calm demeanor. I think he will be a good fit for me."

His friend nodded. "He's the one I would have chosen for you. I think it will be a good match."

I was unsure what it all meant, especially when Sam choked the ball out of my mouth and yanked me back to my kennel to face my earlier poop. I skirted around the pile while fielding questions from Rocko about the *sook* event. I told him that the blue-eyed man had selected me for his team, and he did not intend to kill me. But Rocko was still sure I would be destroyed, dismissing me as gullible; he returned to his pacing.

I lay down in the corner opposite my morning accident, and just as I began to drift off, I caught a whiff of peppermint. My eyes snapped open, and I saw the blue-eyed man sneaking towards me with careful steps, trying not to arouse the other inmates. Our eyes connected as he drew close, and he hunkered down in front of my wire door.

"Hey Turbo," he said. "We are going to be buddies, you and me." His words were soft, like the sigh before a nap.

I watched his gaze shift to the pile in the corner. I waited for disgust to register on his face, but he just looked sad. His fingers hooked over the links of the cage door. "When you're mine, I'm never going to let you sit in shit like that."

There was no anger in his voice. Then he said goodbye, and I watched him walk out the door. I licked the place where his hand had touched the cage, committing his smell to memory.

****

Two weeks of captivity passed. The blue-eyed man had vanished like a field of tennis balls in my dreams. Twelve of the eighteen dogs had been selected, but afterwards, there were no more exhibitions. We returned to the daily grind – meal at night, recess in the morning, the remainder of the day spent in lockdown. Nothing had changed. I began to lose hope that I would ever see the blue-eyed man again.

It was a chilly October morning when a succession of slamming car doors triggered a full bark alert. My ears perked and I sniffed the air for peppermint, but the dogs closest to the main doors reported that the smells were not familiar. The excitement came and went without further incident, and as midday came I was busy checking the air for Sam's cheesy odor, in desperate need of a poop break.

Suddenly the metal doors at the far end of the hall clattered open. King and his pack flooded the halls alongside several men in brown, mottled uniforms that made them look like they were covered in dirt. Several of them seemed disoriented by hundreds of dogs shouting for their attention; the pack moved slowly down the hall, stopping to release dogs along the way. Then the blue-eyed man emerged from the group and started down the hall towards my cage as if on a mission.

A couple of barks leapt out of my throat: *"Here I am!"* I watched recognition spread across his face as he focused in on my kennel. My tail waved hello and I spun in tight circles as he fumbled to unlatch my cage. Finally, the door flew open and I pranced around him as he tried to attach my collar to the leash.

"It's you and me now," he said. "I'm your new Dad." We grinned at each other, and he rubbed the sides of my neck. "Let's go play."

I rushed him outside so we could explore the field. We filtered through the crowd of dogs and new handlers, all of them stepping on each other's feet like an awkward first dance. Many of the handlers were stiff, holding the leashes taut and putting their dogs on guard for an attack. Territories were being established, and tails flagged in ready defense.

Rob, King's lead trainer, yelled: "Just keep them separate from the other dogs… Find your own area, let them get their piss and shit out… Don't give them any commands, just walk them around."

I pulled my new Dad far away from the mob, out to the pastures I had been waiting to search since I arrived. Beyond the parked cars was an old fence post that contained a history of previous dog residents, and I added myself to the list. Then we bounded down a short slope to an old corn silo and trash dump, sniffing for snacks. I investigated droppings of mice, rabbits, and an old badger, as Dad plodded along in tow. He gave me an occasional tug, but mostly allowed me to go about my reconnaissance.

"What's that Turbo? What do you smell?" he asked. And most commonly, "Should you be eating that?" followed by a tug.

A good distance away, Rob was still yelling at the new handlers.

"Just keep bonding with them. Don't give them commands yet. You're gonna put the plastic travel kennels in your vehicles and leave the dogs in the cars during classes. We'll give you some breaks to walk them around more, get to know them."

Dad and I ran back over to the commotion of dogs and

handlers; he sprayed out a small plastic kennel with a hose and wedged it into the back of his truck. Then he looked down at me and asked, "Kennel?" I hopped in and he gave me a head rub.

We drove north, passing fields of green crops and the occasional structure. The buildings multiplied until we reached a bustling town, and exciting new odors seeped through the cracked windows as the car rolled to a stop.

"I'll be right back," Dad said.

I watched him get out of the car and walk away, disappearing through a set of doors that rang a bell. I settled into the floor of my kennel for a restless nap, waking at every jingle and watching people's heads bounce by the car windows. Finally Dad reappeared and walked to the back doors, swinging them open and unlatching my kennel. I greeted him with my nose to sniff the food on his breath.

"Wanna go for a walk?" he asked.

I leapt down onto the asphalt and we made our way down the sidewalk, past open shop doors and through clumps of people. Smells were everywhere – bubble gum, french fries, cigarette butts. I tried to remember them all – grabbing a few for snacks – as I mapped the area. At the pee posts, I sniffed the record of past dogs and left my mark. When I looked back at Dad's grinning face, he seemed to be enjoying our great adventure.

Later that night, Dad moved me into a small kennel house with the other dogs in our pack of "twelve," right next to where the handlers lived. Early the next morning, Dad came back to release me from my cell, and I enjoyed a run in the frosty grass followed by a bowl of kibble and a ride in the car. We drove to a parking lot where Dad met up with the other handlers.

"See you at lunch Turbo," he said before closing the door.

Dad stayed inside of a building with the other handlers while I napped in warm air still trapped in the car. It reminded me of days at the field with Master, waiting for my turn.

At midday Dad and I drove into town to patrol the streets near his lunch spot, returning to King's camp for Dad's afternoon session in the building. When the sun's light had dimmed to rosy pink, he returned to the car and served up a bowl of kibble before we drove out to an empty field – a long stretch of paradise.

He unclipped my leash and whispered, "Now, if I let you go, you're gonna come back, right?"

He had nothing to worry about – he was the best

packmate I'd ever had. I ran until my lungs burned and blood pounded in my ears.

Dad pulled a tennis ball from his pocket and propelled it so high and far that I couldn't beat it to its landing – it bounced twice, and I snagged it and raced back. Seeing another ball in Dad's hand, I dropped the first and sprinted off under the new one's shadow. I ran until I was swallowing gulps of air. Then Dad and I took a break under a big oak tree, catching our breath and watching the sunset behind a drifting cloud of bugs.

When the light faded and the crickets began to sing, we drove back to the kennel house, where we went for one last stroll in the grass before Dad walked me to my cell. The other dogs let out muffled barks while he stroked my neck.

"Goodnight, braaaffy. See you in the morning." Seeing his eyelids droop made mine feel heavy. He closed my kennel door, glancing back one more time before he left the room.

I wanted to cry out – *Take me with you!* But his scent dissipated, and I looked around at the other dogs, lying on the wire floorboards. They had been locked up for hours, all curled up to withstand the chill; their paws were stiff and dry. I was still warm, panting a little; my lungs were still aching from the cold air. I could still smell the tennis ball on my breath. I shut my eyes and relaxed into a deep sleep, muscles still twitching, looking forward to seeing my Dad on the other side.

****

After Dad finished that first week of classroom confinement, our practices resumed. The day opened with breakfast and a walk, and then we met up with the other dogs and handlers for the first block of training. We started with basic orders like *"sit"* and *"aufliggen,"* and then progressed to walking in a *"fooligan"* and *"sooking"* for toys. Dad was new to most of the games –

his eyes often searched his forehead for the words. But he spoke slowly, clearly, giving me a chance to perform, and I quickly learned his language.

Once I taught Dad the basics, our real work began. The tracking trails were long and the scents were sometimes buried; I had to run back and forth a number of times to find the whisper of an odor. Then the track was laid on slippery tile floors and the game reached a whole new level of difficulty.

Our bite games also became more complex. Instead of a suited decoy waiting at the end of a long runway, our opponents began hiding in dark rooms, standing motionless. I sniffed my way to them, nudging the warm fabric for a reaction before clamping down.

My favorite *sook* games were trickier as well. Smells were tucked away on high shelves, out of my reach, their odors falling slowly to the ground. I would pace underneath, jumping up into the scent cone several times before sitting to receive my prize.

Dad was quick and generous with praise, and there was always a tennis ball in his pocket. But the best reward came at the end of our day, when Dad and I would drive out to one of our grassy fields. Alone in the world, he would unclip my leash.

"Go be a puppy," he whispered in my ear.

I would run, so fast my feet hardly touched the ground, and catch the ball as many times as Dad was willing to throw it. Our favorite field – just over the bridge – was a long strip of turf fronting a cold, fast river. I would drop my ball in the water, and the currents would carry it downstream as fast as I could chase it on land. Then I dove in to snag it, leaping out with a shake and racing back to Dad. I would beg him to throw it into the rapids, to launch it as far as he could. I promised him – *I will get it, no matter what.*

When darkness fell around us and the ball was harder to see, we sat for a rest, my muscles cooling quickly in the night air. I would chase the white tails of bunnies and collect the snacks they left behind. Then Dad would give me a *"hoog"* into the back of the car, blasting me with hot air as we drove back to the kennel house. He said goodnight and I settled in – warm, dry, and ready for a long snooze.

****

During our training, the twelve handler-dog pairs were often split into two teams. Our group *sooked* in the morning and did bite work in the afternoon; by the smell of it, the other team practiced the same events in reverse, switching fields while we were gone. One afternoon, we had just finished a set of *sook* games in a junkyard. After finding odors lodged in car parts and piles of trash, the handlers herded us out to the parking lot, where all of the dogs struggled to be the last to pee on the tire propped against the fence.

We hopped in the car and drove several miles northeast, past rows of green stalks. Every time we a passed flat piece of land I whined, "*please can we stop here?*" until it disappeared from sight. Eventually we rolled up in front of an old warehouse, where white paint peeled off the rusted siding. Dad opened the door and I hopped down onto the gravel, sniffing the corn dust.

The last rays of daylight were slipping behind the crops as the other cars parked beside ours. Dogs and dads were conferencing in the lot when Trainer Rob came out of the building to address the group.

"Hey guys, training is running late," he said. "We had a problem with Elvis. After we choked him off a bite, he started having some breathing problems. We monitored him for about half an hour, but his breathing was rough. Sounded like his throat was swelling up. Sam is driving Elvis up to the vet now. He should be calling with an update soon."

The chatter among the dads grew loud as the other team trickled out of the building into the brightness of the floodlight posted atop the door. Some of their faces were sad; others seemed unfazed. They collected into groups, murmuring in concerned tones. Dogs orbited the perimeter, sniffing for food and checking butts; but I stayed close to Dad. I could feel his tension through the leash.

"They had that collar too low on the throat and it crushed his windpipe." Dad muttered to another handler as he pressed his fingers into his own neck.

After several more minutes of shuffling around – and eating a piece of old sandwich crust I found in the dirt – my ears perked at the ring of Rob's telephone. He mumbled a bunch of "mmm-hmms" and "okays" before he made his announcement.

"He didn't make it. Couldn't get any air. They got to the vet too late to save him."

Rob looked down and shrugged, and then shifted his attention back to the warehouse, his face already forgetting. After some grumbling, handlers and dogs started moving into line for our next training event. I looked up at Dad's face – his nostrils were flared. He was about to start barking, and I braced for the eruption.

"Well, that's fucked up," Dad said, loud enough for everyone to hear.

Heads turned. Only the insects continued to buzz.

"That dog died for no good reason," he said. His eyes

surveyed the group and locked onto Rob. "These dogs are our teammates – I consider my dog to be a SEAL."

He motioned down to me, and my head rose.

Dad's eyes flashed towards Elvis's dad and then back to Rob. "We are special ops, and we just let a teammate die because no one here realized that he was having breathing problems. I guarantee you if it was one of us having labored breathing something would have been done. But instead, it took you guys thirty minutes of watching that dog suffer just to make the decision to take him to the vet."

Rob inhaled to respond, but his lips clenched and trapped his voice inside. Dad continued.

"Every one of us here has had advanced medical training. How many people here are the medics for their team?"

A couple of other handlers raised a hand or nodded.

"Yeah, so there is no reason that dog should be dead right now. If someone had just intubated him, created an airway, he would have been fine, even if his windpipe was crushed. You just let a teammate die, and I'm fucking pissed." But his face wasn't angry. It was sad.

No one spoke. Rob's shoulders were hunched and his

jaw was rigid, but he measured Dad and did not even muster a low growl. The other dads shuffled around, averting their eyes and talking about "next time."

When we resumed training, there was an uneasy energy around Dad and me. All eyes were on us. During our game that evening, I brought the fight to the man in the suit until he squeaked for mercy.

We ended that day with a trip to the field by the river. Dad removed two tennis balls from his pocket, and we played catch – as I was on my way back from retrieving the first he'd yell "los," so I dropped that one to start running after the next. When the second ball went missing, I had to hand over the remaining one on Dad's "los" command, holding my breath as he picked up my precious toy; I danced as his arm wrenched back, and then sprinted off to reclaim it. A little bit later that ball disappeared too, and we drove back to the kennel house where Dad tucked me in for the night.

The next evening our team was back at the warehouse for bite training with Trainer Rob. We exited our car and joined the other dads and dogs crunching around the gravel lot. The tension was obvious – eyes were shifty, words curt. Rob and Dad paced around each other like rival lions, keeping their distance. Rob finally vanished inside the building, and Dad and I took our place in line for the bite game, waiting as we listened to other dogs do battle with Billy the pig-scented boy. There were grunts and growls, shoes squeaking on the floor, followed by silence while the dogs were choked off the bite.

We finally reached the front position and I could see the pig boy wearing his jute sleeve, thumping it with his free hand like a catcher's mitt. Dad walked up to Rob, their blood pressures rising. If they had tails both would have been flagging, but Dad's voice came out surprisingly cool.

"Turbo is a KNPV dog," he said. "He has a verbal out. I'm not going to choke him off the bite. I'm just going to give him a *los* command."

Rob took a deep breath and shook his head. "Yeah, he probably does have a verbal out. But I can't let you do it. You need to have positive control over the dog in case he tries to re-attack for safety reasons."

He said the words like an order and stepped away; the issue was closed. But Dad's eyes were defiant. My focus shifted to the pig boy, who was pounding his feet in dramatic fashion.

Dad leaned over and thumped my chest, unclipped my leash, and gave me a quiet *"stellan."* I rushed forward to attack the outstretched arm, digging my teeth through the jute's fibrous weave. His cries were shrill, and his body stiffened as he tried to slip around and give me a mouthful of cushion. I secured the victory, and then, hearing my Dad approach, I braced for the choke; but instead I heard the click of the leash on my collar. Dad took a few steps backwards and said, "*los!*"

I dropped to the ground and Dad led me away from my opponent, who was shaking the pain out of his arm. As we passed Rob, Dad lifted the leash. "Positive control," he said. Rob did not respond.

****

Dad and the other handlers always wore dirt-colored uniforms when we trained. It was the mark of our pack, identifying teammates who were not to be touched. Rob and the other trainers wore black tops and blue jeans – sometimes we were allowed to bite them, but only on handler orders. There were severe penalties for violating these rules, but some dogs needed to test the boundaries.

Bear was a repeat offender. An irritable Dutch Shepherd with the face of a hyena, Bear had spent most of his life in lock-up. All of the humans he'd known had yanked him around, so all he knew was force. He barked spastically before a bite – and he was always threatening to bite something, so he barked constantly. Any intrusion into his territory would trigger one of his rants – fur raised, barks thrusting him backwards like a balloon spitting air.

Bear was the focus of our last class of the day – the one right before Dad and I took our nightly trip to the river – called "socialization." As the sun was setting, the handlers would huddle in a circle under the floodlight. Bear's handler put a muzzle on him and lifted him up with his arms hooked under Bear's belly. Then he passed him to the next handler, who delivered him on to the next, Bear's legs dangling as he endured the handler carousel. He wiggled and screamed threats of destruction each time he was passed to a new set of arms, but the handlers didn't seem to hear or care.

After his socialization classes, Bear was full of rage – he staged all-night barking protests that kept the rest of us awake. But the next night, the dads would muzzle him up again, ignoring his bitching, and pass him around like a bag of food. No matter how many times Bear snarled in their faces, the handlers remained uninterested. They told stories and made football predictions, like they had tuned out his frequency.

Finally, after countless rides, Bear began to suffer his indignity in silence. When the handlers crowded around him at dusk, he accepted the muzzle and braced for the lift. He still objected now and then, but the event had become so routine that it was hard for him to keep up the intensity. Once I caught him listening to the dads' conversation, forgetting for a moment that he was mad.

The handler merry-go-round helped Bear relax around the dads, but he remained suspicious of other dogs. He was insecure, often blowing up at imaginary insults during standard butt sniffs. And because he wasn't the only dog looking for a fight, an exchange of growls would usually lead to a brawl unless one of the handlers was there to break it up. For the most part I avoided Bear. I knew I could take him in battle, but it was easier to just turn on the engines and blast off.

One night, Rob arrived to lead our socialization class. Wearing a thick dark sweatshirt and his typical, angry face, he directed that all the dogs be muzzled. Then the whole pack lined up on a patch of dirt outside the kennel house.

"Lay on the ground next to your dogs, keeping them five feet apart," he instructed.

All of the pairs of dogs and handlers lay down in the dirt. Dad and I were at one end, with Rob shouting right above our heads.

"Now stand up and have Turbo jump over all the other pairs, and then lie down at the other end so the next team can go," Rob instructed.

Dad stood and I scrambled to his side as we stepped up to the first pair.

"Go!"

Dad gave me a "*hoog*," and I leapt over the first pair and ran to the next. By the end of the row we were hurdling at a good clip – quickly enough that by the time I heard the grumblings of dogs accusing me of violating their space, they were already well behind me. But when I tried to jump over Bear, he rose to his feet as I was mid-leap – I heard the snap of his jaws under his mask – and we collided a bit before I sped off. Dad and I cleared the last pair and lay back down in the dirt.

"Good job, *braffy*," Dad whispered.

The next few dogs glided over us, but then it was Bear's turn. At first he refused to perform, barking in protest, as other dogs added their own voices to the ruckus. Bear's handler, holding the leash with both hands, yanked him forward.

Bear started his run, hurdling two pairs before becoming entangled with one of the dogs in the line up, triggering a rapid series of leash yanks. Bear continued the course under threat of revolt; his dad basically had to drag him over the final pair. Bear coughed and snarled as he finished, and his dad pressed him down to the ground.

We played this game five more times; like most pairs,

Dad and I kept getting faster and faster times; we'd all been doing hurdles since we were pups. But Bear became increasingly unstable – and any and all movement set him off.

"You want a piece of me?" he screamed at the backs of our heads as he leapt over top of us.

On every pass, Bear's dad yanked him around, the two of them vying for power. As they rose for their last turn, there were audible groans. Then came the barking – Bear barking at us, his dad barking at him, and Trainer Rob barking at Bear's dad.

"Go over their backs slower, and every time Bear even looks at one of those dogs, give him a strong correction and yell *fooey.*"

Bear successfully contained his rage as he jumped over the first three pairs, but he had a meltdown over the fourth.

"*Fooey!*" his dad screamed. He jerked the leash so hard that it pulled Bear off the course. They both stood off to the side, dazed and panting.

Rob strode up to Bear's dad, his voice low. "This is what we are going to do. If he does it again, you string that fucking dog up. Choke him until he almost stops moving, and then put him down and immediately tell him to *aufliggen.* You need to let that dog know who's boss – let him know that you are in charge. Impose your will."

Bear started the course again, remaining on task until he reached the second to last dog. There were a few low growls, and then a declaration of war; Bear roared and bucked backwards like a horse.

That's when his dad yanked him into the air – the whole pack went silent, all heads turning to see Bear's feet dangling above the ground, his eyes ballooning in fear. He kicked off of his dad's leg, trying to secure a foothold; but the leash swung backwards, and the collar wrenched down tighter on his neck. He writhed and wiggled until panic paralyzed him. The rage drained out of him along with his energy. Just as I was expecting twitches, his dad dropped him – he hit the ground and wavered to his feet, blinking to focus his eyes.

Rob nodded his approval to Bear's dad, who seemed as drained and disillusioned as Bear. We finished the event, and Dad and I walked to our car in silence.

Dad and I raised our spirits with a trip to the field, where I ran extra fast after the ball to stay warm. We arrived at the kennel later that night; Dad said goodnight and I curled up to sleep, trying not to listen to Bear's whimpers. After that day, Bear became distant – he hardly seemed to recognize any of us anymore.

Chapter 4
San Diego

When I met Dad his face was bare. As we drove to the airport, reddish-brown fur was creeping across his chin and neck. I sat in the back of the car, surrounded by bags, watching tall buildings pass in the windows – we were leaving King's school to find new adventures.

We pulled up to a long concrete field; Dad gave our car away and struggled to load our gear onto a bus while I searched for snacks, having skipped breakfast. We arrived at the shiny terminal, where Dad loaded our bags on a cart and we rolled up to a line of people, taking our place at the end. Some people near me smiled, others averted their eyes. Dad shuffled papers around at the counter, while I sniffed the marble wall, learning about the thousands who had come before us.

Dad handed over our equipment, and then we explored the terminal – outdoors first, where Dad reminded me every few steps to "go potty." I went on the base of a planter and tugged him back inside where it was warm – full of commotion and slippery floors, the scents of cinnamon and coffee.

"What a beautiful dog. What kind is he?" people asked Dad. He would smile and say "Dutch Shepherd," as they reached down to pat my neck, and I sniffed their pockets for snacks. Dad never let me accept their offerings.

When it was time to board the plane, Dad walked me to my kennel. "We are going home, buddy," he said. "To San Diego. It's warm there. We are going to run on the beach, and swim in the ocean... You will love it, I promise."

Men wearing thick waist straps loaded my kennel onto their cart and we rode over the cold acres of concrete to the plane. I was lifted into the underbelly, where I curled into a ball for a fitful sleep.

On the other end of the trip Dad greeted me with water and snacks. We defrosted inside the terminal, gathered our bags, and then slipped through the glass doors into the crisp night air. A car stopped, and a woman popped out and ran over to Dad. After they nuzzled a bit, Dad introduced us.

"Here he is, this is Turbo. Turbo, this is your new mommy."

She kneeled down next to me. She smelled sweet, but it wasn't real – there was no food in her pockets. She gave me a few careful pets and scratched under my chin.

"Hi, sweetheart. It's nice to meet you."

I couldn't find a trace of tennis ball on her clothes, so I lost interest in her, but she seemed to come with the car. I kept my eyes on Dad to make sure I went wherever he was going. He gave me a *"hoog"* and I jumped in the back with the bags and my kennel, scanning for a good park where we could stop to play a game of catch.

****

San Diego's salty sea air reminded me of Holland, but the breeze was warmer, and the dirt was dry and hard. My new kennel house was a small concrete facility, with a yard for peeing and a large training field just a short distance away down a gravel road. Checking in, I was introduced to the three other residents – Hammer, Loki, and Storm.

Hammer was a tall Dutch Shepherd with faded stripes across his belly. He barked a hoarse hello when I entered, and proclaimed himself the veteran of our crew. Loki, a cranky, golden Belgian, was also a long time resident. He reported several crimes he'd witnessed, but most of them sounded like nonsense to me. My third neighbor, Storm, was a shiny black German Shepherd – the only dog I'd ever met that could keep up with me in a sprint.

Storm was next in line for the "deployment" tournament, where Hammer and Loki had already been competitors more than once. A few days after I arrived, a Belgian Malinois named Diesel joined our crew – he had a thick coat, a strong jaw, and preferred a belly rub to a ball any day.

Training days in San Diego started at dawn, when a seagull stationed in the palm tree would alert us to the arrival of the first dad. Bowls of kibble were dispensed, and then each of us was released one by one, while the others watched from their cells. For my recess I enjoyed a morning sprint to chase off the bunnies, which usually triggered one of Loki's fits. Storm and Diesel spent their free time cuddling with the dad on duty, trying to get in position for a butt scratch. Loki and Hammer patrolled the kennels during their breaks, barking complaints at captive neighbors and pissing on cage fronts.

The sound of Dad's car pulling up gave me the spins. I heard his hasty steps, the clink of the gate, all of it leading up to our joyous reunion. We spent every day together – training, playing catch, and afterwards, finding an empty strand of beach where I could sprint through the surf and prove that the waves couldn't catch me.

We played the same games I'd practiced for years, but with a few new elements added. We played more in dark warehouses, where I had to rely on my nose and ears to find the bite target. Even when I found my opponent, sometimes he would be hiding in rafters or behind doors where I couldn't reach him to get a bite. I finally barked in frustration, and then I'd get a whiff of Dad and a rousing thump on my chest. "Thaat's a good boy! That's my good *braffy!*" he whispered.

We also practiced a lot of "*sooking*" – mostly off-leash. My nose led me around buildings and fields searching for bomb odors with Dad close on my heels, and I won every time, sitting next to the source to receive my tennis ball reward. I liked to chew them until the insides popped, and tear off their fuzzy yellow covers.

On Friday mornings all of the dads arrived early, when the sky was still purple. We would line up on the beach and march into the freezing ocean, dads and dogs alike whining when the water reached our genitals. We walked into the surf until our feet didn't touch, and paddled with numb legs to a small island that was covered in pelicans, our approach causing a mass exodus of birds. We took a few steps onto the mushy sandbar before turning around and heading back to shore. Storm and I would race back to the beach, leaping out to spray each other as we shook out our coats.

Less fun were the days when we had to climb tall buildings, and be thrown off the other side. Loki and Hammer warned that the dads would try to kill us this way, but I thought they were delusional – like my old neighbor Rocko, who always warned of imminent executions.

Sure enough, a few days later Dad strapped me to his back and began climbing a ladder... higher, higher... so dangerously high that I panicked. I tried to wiggle out of the straps and leap off his back, but he caught me and we dangled for a moment, staring down at the ground far below, our hearts racing. Dad finally managed to shift our weight back and get us up the ladder and onto the roof. He gave me a few minutes with a tennis ball to relax before wrapping me in a vest, attaching it to a rope, and lowering me to the ground as the straps dug into my leg-pits... definitely not my favorite game.

I was also introduced to a helicopter – Dad called it a "hee-lo" – which is a machine that looks like a dragonfly. We crawled into its belly and it screamed as it lifted straight up into the air. A second later we were flying next to the birds, the brushy hills rushing past us. Suddenly, Dad looked over at me.

"You ready, Turbo?"

I searched his face for clues. *Ready for what?* He clipped my vest to his waist, grabbed hold of a rope, and we jumped out, zipping towards the ground. Wind whipped my face and the vest hugged my chest, making it hard to breathe. Loki, who was right behind me, cursed the whole way down. We slowed just before we hit the ground, and other dogs and dads followed in quick succession, stepping down onto a barren patch of desert.

I was happy to be alive, to feel the grains of sand

sticking to my pads. Meanwhile right behind me, Loki was still bitching about these "suicide missions," and Hammer, riled up by Loki, was plotting his revenge. They taunted me with I told you so's, but I was still pretty sure Dad wasn't trying to kill me.

Once we had mastered the new regimen, Dad and I started travelling by van or airplane to new stadiums for "away" games. I loved these trips – Dad and I were together all the time, training at night, and sleeping in a soft bed into the afternoon. We spent our free hours playing tug with a jute bar, or touring the block near our hotel. Sometimes Dad took me to restaurants and I would lie under the table, sniffing for fallen scraps as I watched the pigeons strut by.

Other SEALs joined us for the away games; some Dad already knew, others we'd just met. They were all members of our pack who wore the same dirt-colored uniforms. We competed in fast-paced events – running, ducking, and shooting guns at opponents that wore long, fluttery dresses over their bite pads. My portion of the event still involved hunting for bombs and chasing down bite targets when they darted out of hiding spots. Our new packmates supported my work, celebrating my finds and pointing out where my opponent had run – my victories earned points for the whole team.

On one of our trips, we arrived at a tarmac under a

gray sky that covered everything with a fine, wet mist. The fields beyond the airport were lush and quiet; it reminded me of Holland. We checked into our hotel room for a short nap and then drove out to a large auditorium to meet up with the rest of the guys. The pack was busy planning the night's game as I roamed the rows of chairs, checking hands for snacks when they reached out to pet me.

Finally we moved outside, where the pack put on goggles that allowed them to see in the dark. I was attached to Dad walking lead, and I could smell the pack walking behind us – whiffs of corn-cereal, tobacco-spit, hair gel, and candy. We began hiking into a densely wooded area, quietly making our way through the tangle of brush and hopping over felled trees. Then the radio devices crackled to life and the game commenced; the pack ran, angled, and dropped to the ground. Someone would scream, *"contact left!"* and all of the guns would erupt in concert, rattling my innards.

On the first practice run, I was standing next to Dad while the packs' guns pounded at an empty hilltop. One by one, our packmates stopped shooting to run past us to a new spot, where they would flop back down on their bellies and continue firing downrange. The hair gel-scented man just to our right stood up and began running in our direction, raising his hand in the air and threatening to hit Dad in the back.

"Last man!" he yelled as his arm swung down – I lunged. I would have gotten a piece of him if Dad hadn't spun me around with my leash, yanking me back to the ground.

"*Fooey!*" Dad yelled.

The three of us were all a little stunned. Then Dad and the hair gel man laughed.

"Yeah, we are definitely going to have to spend some time working on that one," Dad said.

The game paused, and the pack lined up several yards away with their guns pointed in the air; then Dad got down on his belly as I stood guard. I watched one of our mates run up, his arm winding up to hit Dad's back, and I wanted to strike him – but I could feel tension in the leash.

"*Bliven*," Dad said, his tone serious. I knew I would get a yank if I moved, so I sat and watched each member of the pack slap Dad on the back and run off. Apparently it was all part of their game.

We continued playing until almost sun-up – the pack lying on their bellies to shoot, then popping up and running – it was a series of movements that they all knew by heart. I ran alongside Dad, panting until my tongue was dry.

The next night we started with a *sook* practice. The pack wasn't competing in the event, but they came to watch me sniff. As we entered the rooms of a new building, they walked behind Dad – some chattering, rooting me on; all of them knocking around like a bunch of puppies. No matter how hard they tried to distract me, the promise of the tennis ball kept me on target – I won match after match.

Later that night we played a round of bite games with the pack in attendance – this time they were silent as a puffy-suited man emerged at the end of a hallway, banging around like an angry gorilla. I launched and caught his shoulder in my teeth, whipping him back and forth – the pack went wild, whooping and hollering with every jerk. After the tussle Dad said *"los,"* and I ran back to him, proudly receiving pats on the head from all my guys.

For our final set of games that evening, the pack lined up next to the exterior wall of a building, with Dad and I positioned closest to the entrance. Our padded opponent appeared, teasing me with a little dance before running back inside the structure, daring me to chase him. My legs pulsated as I awaited the command; finally, Dad unclipped my leash.

"Find em!"

I sprinted inside with the pack on my tail, and tracked

our opponent's stink to a room where I attacked
his arm; we wrestled until he surrendered and Dad
declared me the victor. In other rooms, my packmates
were shooting rounds into cardboard figures, racking
up even more points. Once we had conquered all of
the opponents and cardboard, I did a final *sook* for
bombs to close out the event.

Exhausted from a long night of surging adrenaline,
the pack returned to the warm auditorium, where we
filled our bellies with food and water. My packmates
removed their gear and lounged back in their chairs
to let their rotten feet dry. As they talked through the
debrief, I circled the room begging for one last ball toss
before curling up on the threadbare carpet, lulled to
sleep by the sound of my brothers.

****

Back home in San Diego, Dad was obsessed with
books and videos about dog training – and the more he
learned, the more arguments he got into with Trainer
Pete.

Trainer Pete was our main instructor in San Diego. He
reminded me of Trainer Sam – upbeat, friendly, and a
casual choker. Dad argued that yanking collars during
matches was ineffective and confusing, that it made
the dogs anxious; but Trainer Pete pointed to veterans
like Loki and Hammer, who didn't seem to notice they

were being jerked around unless it knocked them off-balance.

After a few of their blowouts, training started to change, with each dog practicing the bite game by different rules depending on his dad. Hammer and Loki wore bulky shock collars, while Storm and Diesel paired a leather collar with a choke chain. I just wore the leather.

When Trainer Pete appeared on the field in the puffy bite suit, we knew it was time to play. Hammer was first up – a tall dog with oversized jaws, and bite was his best skill. He barked taunts downfield until he received his command, and then sped off to hit Trainer Pete hard, knocking him backward. Once on the bite, Hammer shook and grunted, trying with every bit of strength to rip the padding off the arm.

The match was over when Hammer's dad said "los," but Hammer never let go upon hearing the command. Soon, waves of electricity would start flowing into his neck – his eyes widened – and he would steel himself against the pain. But eventually the effort of resistance wore him out and he released his grip, dropping to the ground. There was no celebration – he was not the clear winner.

Loki was another brawler. The sight of Trainer Pete in his gear made him froth at the mouth – he would strain against the leash, whining, snarling, so excited that he could barely hear the commands. When he felt the leash release he flew at Trainer Pete, attacking with his own special kind of crazy. His bites were sloppy but dramatic, shallow and desperate. His game was less about strategy than deliverance.

After a short, violent tussle, Loki's dad yelled "*los*," but Loki thought the word meant "surrender" and he flatly refused, preparing to receive the first of several jolts. The shocks gave his growls a rapid vibrato, and his hair stood on end. Finally the jolts weakened his grip and he fell, growling and snapping at the air around him as his dad pulled him back to his kennel.

Storm had a nervous approach to bite matches. He was a great athlete but his bite was weak – he relied on his long canines to do most of the damage. His first match against Trainer Pete was a tentative dance, and when it was over Storm heard his dad command him to "*los*," but he was afraid of what would happen if he let go. Irritated, his dad whipped his butt with a leash yelling "*los*," but Storm stood frozen on the bite.

Finally his dad choked him off, and Storm figured that he had lost the match. After several frustrating drills, Storm began spinning around Trainer Pete when he heard his dad approaching, whining, "*What am I doing wrong?*" He was relieved when his turn was over, and the next dog was called up from the pen.

Diesel and I had a similar style. Our initial bite was deep – we wanted our opponent to know that the beating would be over more quickly if they submitted. When it was his turn to play, Diesel tackled Trainer Pete and held him down with his low center of gravity and fast rear end. He was a beast on the bite, blessed with a massive set of jaws – Trainer Pete whimpered as he struggled to regain his footing. But when the "los" command came Diesel ignored it, and after several rounds of being choked off the bite, he started to adopt Storm's spin move to avoid his dad.

When Dad brought me to the launch zone, I examined Trainer Pete with an eye to predict and punish his movements. Dad leaned down and thumped my chest.

"Yeah, *br-r-raffy… stellan!*"

I sped down the course at Trainer Pete, like a shark moving through water. He took a step back as I catapulted toward him, hitting his left shoulder and grinding my teeth into the form beneath the padding. He groaned and tried to shake me off – slapping at me, spinning me around, and knocking me into walls.

Trainer Pete submitted, and Dad told me to "*los.*" I usually let go right away – we practiced *los* constantly – but there was one particularly good round when I pleaded for more time. He ran up and praised me.

"Good boy! Yaah, *br-r-raffy*. You got him."

Then he gave me another "*los*," slipping his hand under my collar as a warning. I dropped.

Back at the kennels after that night's bite practice, Hammer and Loki complained about their dads' mixed signals – ordering them to fight and then punishing them with a choke for a job well done. In the cage next door to mine, Storm pouted quietly. Diesel had fallen asleep right after dinner – the only motion in his cage was an occasional paw twitch.

I finally dozed off as well, dreaming about bite matches and Dad cheering me on from the sidelines. Sometime during the night I heard rustling, whispers; Storm being let out of his cage. I awoke the next morning to find that he was gone – off to compete in the deployment tournament in Afghanistan.

****

When we weren't practicing, Dad and I went to the
beach. He sat in a chair and read about dog training
while I balanced my ball at the very top of a sand berm
and let it roll down towards the ocean – gaining speed,
faster and faster – as the waves threatened to steal it
out to sea. I would rescue it at the last possible second,
my tail wagging in relief.

After Dad's studies, he liked to test his new methods –
his favorite was clicker training. He gave me obedience

commands, and when I performed them correctly he made a "click" sound and handed me a piece of food. It was an easy game with lots of snacks, so I was always down to play.

Dad talked to the other dads about his new ideas – usually while I was trying to get him to throw a tennis ball – but many argued that this approach would "take too long" and required "too much change." It wasn't until Dad and I demonstrated a steady reign of game supremacy that some of the other dads started trying out Dad's system of clicks and food instead of chokes.

One hot afternoon, we drove an hour east into the desert to practice bite work on men who wore long dresses over their pads. Each dog was released to "*find*" these men and "*stellan*" them, while the rest of us watched from our cars and waited our turn. During my round, I searched down trails and through ravines looking for padded opponents with Trainer Pete following me around, shooting a gun into the air. It was an irritating distraction, but I ignored him.

When it was Hammer's turn to run the event, the gunshots rang in his ears – and he couldn't take it. Years of training and deployments had made him sensitive to explosions; he only searched a few yards before he threw a full-blown tantrum, completely abandoning the game.

The last session of the day was devoted to desensitizing Hammer to the sound of gunfire. Trainer Pete stood next to Hammer, who was attached to his Dad's leash, and opened fire – a stream of sharp blasts. Hammer went crazy, snarling and yowling, while his dad yanked on his neck and yelled *"fooey!"* It was a mix of chaos and torture.

Finally, Trainer Pete stopped firing and Hammer stopped screaming; there was a pause while Trainer Pete talked to Hammer's dad. Then Trainer Pete fired another shot – Hammer again demanded the noise stop, and in response his dad yanked his neck hard. After several more rounds of this *bang*-bark-yank game, Hammer was so incensed that he bit his dad on the leg.

There was blood on the breeze when Dad opened the car door to get out, grabbing my snacks bag. "Stupid… stressing this dog out…" he mumbled, and closed the door behind him. He walked over and took Hammer's leash, tied it to a shade tree, and then marched back to bark at Trainer Pete. Their voices rose and fell before Dad grabbed the gun and shoved the snacks bag in the hand of Hammer's dad.

"Timing is important here!" Dad shouted as he stomped down a path separating the fields of brush – then he fired a single shot. Before Hammer could protest, his dad shoved a palm-full of snacks at his face. Hammer scarfed them down, and his dad's hand brushed over his head.

Dad moved closer as he fired several more shots – and every time there was a sharp crack, Hammer's dad shoved a treat in his face. Finally, Dad walked back and handed the gun to Hammer's dad, who shot one last burst of rounds high over Hammer's head before giving a very focused Hammer his final treat – gunfire had become his dinner bell.

Later that week we were practicing *sook* at the shed down the road from our kennel house. It was a simple game where balls popped out of a wooden wall, but Loki was having one of his meltdowns – he had located a hint of cherry-scented bombs and become antsy, stomping his feet and demanding a reward. The game required us to sit down near the source, but Loki wanted to be ready to leap when the ball popped out of the wall.

His dad ordered him to *"sit,"* but Loki danced around, his eyes flashing to the wall. Trainer Pete directed Loki's dad to give him a yank but it hardly fazed Loki, who was still expecting a ball to appear any second.

After another failed command and another hard correction, Dad stood up, shaking his head – he and Trainer Pete engaged in another debate.

"This makes no sense," Dad shouted. "We need these dogs to find bombs in Afghanistan, so in that dog's mind, this should be the best game in the whole world. He should want to play it all the time. When you start yanking his neck, he isn't going to think bomb detection is fun – and if he stops thinking it's fun, we are going to get blown up."

After his clash with Trainer Pete, Dad pulled Loki outside and began giving him snacks, not asking him to do anything in return – just making a "click" sound before he handed over each reward. Loki was hypnotized, and happily accepted the food.

"*Sit*," Dad ordered, and Loki instantly complied. When his butt touched the ground, there was a "click" and another treat. They played several times – by the end, Loki played even when Dad only gave him a click and praise.

Once Loki was eager to *sit* on command, Dad took him back to the game course where Loki's dad commanded him to "*sook!*" Loki quickly found the odor and pranced around, his butt bobbing above the ground.

"*Sit*," Loki's dad ordered, and Loki's butt slammed to the floor. The ball was revealed, and Loki greedily chewed his reward. Loki finally understood why *sook* was my favorite – a choke-free game with toys and treats.

Several months later, Dad was winning his battle with Trainer Pete, but they suddenly stopped arguing – Dad was distracted by the need to make piles. He made mountains of game gear that included vests, leashes, collars, balls, and enormous bags of food. Then he began putting those piles into large plastic boxes and green canvas bags. Reddish fur grew thick on his face. We were the next team going to Afghanistan, where the great "deployment" competition was held.

One day, Storm returned to the kennel. I wasn't sure how he'd fared in the games, but he did not have the proud strut of a champion. His attention span was short, and he had developed uncomfortable nervous ticks. He paced in his kennel, often alerting the rest of us to things he saw scurrying into the shadows. He whined about explosions, and how the humans were going to kill us. It was like living next to Rocko all over again.

The whole crew was reunited for about a week before Hammer disappeared; and a few days later, Dad and I left too, following Hammer out to the deployment games.

Chapter 5
Afghanistan

Mom dropped us off at the airfield at dawn; her eyes were puffy. She and Dad nuzzled many times before the propellers of the C-130 could be heard approaching over the eastern mountains. I sniffed the concrete, inhaling dust, trying to find anything edible. As usual, my belly was empty before our plane ride, and Dad kept repeating the word "potty," and begging me to pee on everything.

I lay in my kennel during most of the long flights; every once in a while Dad and I toured the cabin, meeting other passengers who stroked my head as I searched their bags for food. In between flights, we had short stops in new locales where we sniffed and peed.

On our third day of travel, the plane landed on a flat expanse of shimmering heat. Dad and I stepped out onto the tarmac, where vapors of jet fuel coated my sinuses and filled my lungs. Scanning this place called Afghanistan, I could not find a single patch of grass to play ball on, and the smell of stewing waste warned of the blazing temperatures coming in the days ahead.

Dad loaded our gear into a truck and we drove to the part of camp that would become our stomping grounds, where we were assigned to an air-conditioned plywood room with a single bunk, a desk and some shelves. There was a flap in the door that led to an outdoor wire kennel with an asphalt floor and a fabric cover for shade – I hoped to never see the inside of it.

We hurried inside the cool room, and I hopped up to lay on the bunk as Dad carried in boxes of gear, unpacked bags, hung lights around the room, and draped our game uniforms onto wall hooks. He arranged his books and computer on the plank desk in the corner, and piled our bedding beside me. My sleep pad was tucked into a strip of floor next to my food and water bowls.

Once our room was set up, Dad and I walked one building over to visit Hammer; I could see him curled up in the outdoor cage as we approached, his dark coat absorbing the sun's rays. We found Hammer's dad inside the refrigerated room that looked just like ours, and then we went back outside to release Hammer from his cell.

While our dads talked, Hammer and I cruised the courtyard, and I could see the exhaustion in his face. He complained of long, sleepless nights; panting but never getting cool. A week in Afghanistan had already put years of wear and tear on his angular frame. His skin seemed to be melting off his bones.

After an hour spent standing on the scalding asphalt, we walked back to our air-cooled room and I leapt up on the bunk to watch Dad make piles again. He ventured outside into the broiling sun and returned with armfuls of equipment – then he spent the rest of the day sorting and organizing, scooping the piles of gear into backpacks and preparing our game vests for an upcoming match.

We only had one sunset to enjoy our new digs before we were scheduled to go on our first "op" – a series of events in the ongoing tournament of games. Following a restless sleep interrupted by distant rumbles, Dad and I joined our SEAL pack the next afternoon to plan the night's events. Tobacco-spit man, candy man and the others received me warmly with pets and friendly chest thumps. We gathered in a long conference room, where I tried to propose a game of tug or catch. When that idea was rejected, I checked the trashcans for snacks; then Dad barked "*auff*," and I lay down on the gritty carpet while the pack discussed the night's adventures.

Dad returned from our meeting full of energy. We feasted on a big meal and went for a "potty" walk – I kept asking Dad whether he had a ball in his pocket, but he said it was not time to play. We returned to our room and Dad checked all of our gear, confirming that the piles were in the proper bags before turning his attention back to me.

"Let's get you ready."

He snapped a collar around my neck and helped me into my vest, attaching several gadgets for me to carry; then he put on his own vest and heaved a massive pack onto his shoulders. With my leash clipped on we walked out into the dark night, towards the glow of a fire in a metal barrel where the pack had gathered; I inspected hands for food and tennis balls.

The buses arrived, and we climbed in; Dad "*hooged*" me into a seat and stood next to me, his arm latched onto a bar overhead. The buses rolled over to an airfield, and we hopped down onto the dimly lit tarmac. The pack walked to a spot and lied on a carpet of rocks, still warm from the day's heat, where we listened to the scream of planes taking off. Some of our packmates plugged music into their ears as they stared up into the sky; there was an occasional ripple of chuckles.

I heard the drubbing of helicopters moving towards us, invisible in the night sky; they whisked up the dust and rocks around us when they touched down. Dad covered me with his body until it calmed, and then we hopped into the rear of the bug behind our team.

My heart pounded, and I could hear the rest of the pack's hearts thumping in concert. Even the helicopter seemed excited, with its shrill whine and its rotors pumping us to our destination. The rising energy was driving me to spin, but Dad hugged me to him.

"*Sit!*" he whispered. "Thaaat's a good boy. It's okay buddy. You just relax."

We moved northwest for about an hour, catching glimpses of a twin helicopter that carried the rest of the pack through the gap in our bug's rear hatch. The two machines hovered and swung over the valley floor, abruptly pulling in the reins to fly up the face of a mountain, and then careening down the other side. We finally set down in a bowl, surrounded by tall peaks. The team scrambled off the bird and leapt to the ground in a fog of dust; the helos disappeared, their screams trailing off over the horizon.

Dad hooked me to the long leash attached to his waist. Our pack huddled for a head count before moving east through the towering rocks. We walked quickly, climbing over jagged terrain, our feet kicking up puffs of sand that stuck to our sweaty faces. We followed a path towards a mountain peak for several minutes – then we heard a blast that detonated just to our left.

The explosion reverberated around the silent valley. The pack stopped, scanning our surroundings with night-vision goggles and whispering into radios. The shot was ruled "recon by fire" – a test by our opponents to see if we were ready to start the games. We continued moving forward.

More bangs erupted from our left; something flew towards us, cracking high above our heads. Dad stopped momentarily, scanning the hills; the pack paused to deliberate and then continued moving, more swiftly now.

We had not covered much ground when the whole world opened up. There was an orchestra of blasts on our left and right – short, high tones overlapping with big, low vibrations that rocked the innards. Long whooshes passed and landed on the hills above us, combusting the air. The pack charged forward, up a rocky path towards a wall of rocks. The game had begun.

Dad was running toward a large boulder, and I
struggled to keep up, leaping over rocks twice my size.
Snaps and pops sprayed my feet with shards of stone,
and a fireball hit the boulder ahead of me, warming my
face. I was trying to catch up to Dad, who was diving
behind the large boulder, as explosions crashed all
around me – when suddenly Dad yanked me so hard
by my neck I flew all the way to the rock, my shoulder
hitting him in his knees and knocking us both to the
ground. I whined from the pain, stunned by the hard
correction.

Dad grabbed me around the waist and pulled me
behind the boulder before I could regain my balance.
Once I was back on my feet, I scanned Dad's face for
reassurance – *had I done something wrong?* – but he was
distracted, busy shooting his gun at our opponents.
The pounding was so intense, I couldn't tell who was
winning.

Pops of light showered the rocks around us – the
explosions were close enough to feel hot gusts of air,
thick with reward-worthy odors. The pack leapt up in
unison and ran quickly down a hill; I sprinted to stay
with Dad, ignoring pain in my neck and pads. With
our bodies hugging the cliff face, we hustled towards
the mountain at the far end of the valley. The pops
behind us finally grew faint, and the pack stopped to

return our opponents' gunfire.

The radios gurgled, and soon I heard the welcome whine of the helicopters. The sky erupted with thuds and explosions, igniting the mountains around us in flames. We sprang forward through the illuminated valley, the pack moving in familiar patterns, shooting and running. Dad and I were slipping over rocks and boulders, our hearts pounding. We hit the incline of the eastern mountain, hurdling rock crevasses as we climbed. Volleys of gunfire echoed along the valley walls.

Just before we reached the crest of the mountain, silence blanketed the basin behind us; we hunkered down behind a slab of boulders to rest. My tongue was so dry and crusted I felt as if I'd lapped up a mouthful of dirt; I caught my breath while Dad dug through his bag and pulled out a bowl that he filled with water from a tube on his shoulder. I gulped it down, relieved by its coolness, and swallowed a handful of kibble as Dad guzzled water from his shoulder tube and squeezed a packet of syrup into his mouth. I tried to sniff the wrapper for leftovers, but we were already back on the move.

Dad and I took the lead, and he ordered me to "*sook*" down the other side of the mountain. Panting hard, I inhaled the odors around us – plants and dust, nothing worthy of reward.

We reached flat ground and approached a structure made of mud, hay, and goat dung. The sky was dark and quiet; our ears were still ringing from the blasts. The pack was tense, scanning the area for movement. Dad commanded me to *sook* the compound walls, and I ran the perimeter with my nose to the ground, but found nothing. I returned to Dad and we posted up at the heavy wooden door, waiting for the next phase of the game to commence. The pack fidgeted behind us, ready with their guns.

The "terp" – a member of our pack who spoke our opponents' language – began explaining the game rules to the people inside the compound, followed by a series of demands. Moments later, the wooden door opened and a flock of women and children shuffled out. I sniffed their group – irritation, fear, no bombs. They were guided to the far side of the compound, where a packmate guarded them as they milled around like nervous lambs.

More announcements by the terp prompted a crowd of men to filter out. They raised their shirts at the end of our gun barrels; then the pack fastened their hands behind their backs, and directed them to a separate area where they could be examined. Our pack's terp made some final declarations before Dad walked me up to the open wooden door.

"Find 'em!"

I ran inside, sniffing the stale air trapped within the walls for an odor that might lead me to a bite. With my pack in tow, I darted from room to room, surrounded by the smells of our opponents – goat oils, sharp herbs and musk. The rest of the pack searched rooms just behind me, their guns extending from their noses. We found no *stellan*-worthy targets, but Dad gave me a pat on the neck and thump to the chest. "Good job, *braffy*."

After confirming that none of our opponents had stayed behind to play, Dad gave me a *"sook,"* and I circled back through the rooms. In the third one I entered, I caught a hint of explosives behind rolled floormats that led me to a metal trunk buried underneath heaps of books. Dad gave me a quick, *"here!"* just as my butt started lowering into a sit, and I ran to accept my ball, chewing happily as one of our pack members investigated the trunk. Inside he found four long pipe bombs, which he carefully placed into a large rucksack for transport.

I checked the rest of the compound without any more finds. As the pack continued to inspect the rooms, the radios reported that a "squirter" was fleeing the village, heading northeast. Dad and I ran outside with six other members of our pack, and we gathered near an orchard of fig trees, all of us jittery with adrenaline.

Surveying our crew, Dad whispered, "The wind is moving south to north, so we're going to patrol out along the downwind flank of the orchard. When Turbo picks up the scent I'm going to cut him loose for the bite. You'll hear screaming, and then we'll rush in and grab the guy. Stay close – and no matter what, do not shoot my dog."

Dad ordered me to "*find em*," and I raced forward, dragging him behind me. Detecting some human scent on a northern wind current, I made a hard right and started tugging Dad between two rows of trees, the mud sucking at our feet. Then Dad reeled me back in and unclipped my leash.

"*Stellan!*" he whispered.

I darted deep into the shadows, chasing the scent of sweat and catching a glimpse of a figure ahead shifting through low branches that rustled in his wake. I tracked the sound of his frantic steps until I was close enough to feel his body heat; his head turned at the thump of my feet behind him, but his eyes scanned the space above my head.

I sprung, hitting him in the back of his shoulder and knocking us both to the ground. He yelped as my teeth crushed through fabric and muscle, and I could feel his heart pounding, vibrating my incisors. He squirmed, screaming, and began punching my ribs and kicking my hindquarters.

I was surprised by his strength – his hits were landing and they hurt. I cried through my clenched teeth, trying to dodge his strikes and whipping him off balance. He became increasingly desperate, clawing at my face and grabbing handfuls of my skin, twisting and wrenching. For one horrible moment, I considered the possibility that he could win.

Then the pack appeared, their weapons pointed at my opponent's head. Two of them descended on top of him, binding his hands together.

"*Los!*"

I heard Dad's order but I held on, waiting to feel my opponent go limp. Dad repeated the command to release him, and I growled as I nibbled my way off. I guarded Dad, daring my opponent to make a move.

We rejoined the rest of the pack, and our packmates took my opponent away for an examination. Dad checked my legs and cleaned the gashes and scratches, then we trekked out of the village, Dad and I walking point – I *sooked* for bombs as we moved up a path towards another set of buildings, their outlines barely visible in the moonlight.

My ears perked when I heard an opponent dart out of a structure ahead – the shuffle of footsteps finding traction in the dirt. A heartbeat later, Dad's gun fired and I heard the thud of our opponent hitting the ground. My ears turned towards another set of footsteps, creeping slowly, but before I could pinpoint the location there was a series of gun blasts – I heard a fall, followed by twitching in the dirt. As we approached the bodies, I could smell their sweet, warm gases escaping. A pack member kicked guns away from their jittery hands and collected the game equipment and papers hidden inside their clothes.

We reached the compound and Dad had me "*sook*" the exterior for bombs. Finding no scores, he nudged me through a doorway.

"*Find em!*" he said in my ear.

I tore through the rooms, the pack on my tail. I searched furniture, dusty floor mats, pans, a stove, burlap sacks, and metal boxes, but found only typical smells – no humans hiding. Dad instructed me to "*sook*," but none of their game equipment had been left behind.

The pack converged in the courtyard, their facial expressions coming into focus in the pre-dawn light. Packmates talked into the crackling radios as occasional gun pops echoed through the otherwise peaceful valley. A decision was made to claim the compound, and our guys began removing their game equipment, settling into the enemy's lair. Dad gave me two bowlfuls of water and tied my leash to a post; I sniffed within range and peed in the corner while Dad helped the pack fill bags with dirt. A few packmates climbed onto the roof, mounting guns on the building's corners.

The sun had barely cleared the horizon when a chorus of blasts began – dust and smoke rose from a cluster of bullets landing in the courtyard. Dad pulled me into a stuffy room, tying me to a post next to the grilling pit where the smell of meat in the ash taunted me as I listened to a volley of cracks and booms being exchanged. Every few minutes, a blast hit so hard that dust rained from the ceiling, coating me in powder. It sounded as though the earth was being ripped apart, threatening to split in two.

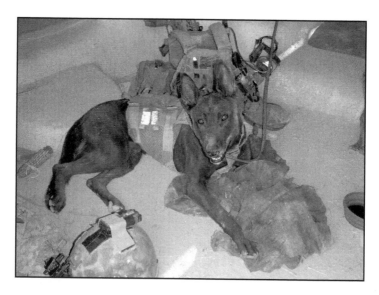

I lay there on a soot-covered rug at the doorway, listening to our building get pummeled by rockets. Then the helicopters came, swooping in to turn the tide. I perked up at every noise, in hopes that it was Dad... but as hours passed and temperatures swelled, I drifted in and out of consciousness.

When the sun was at the highest point in the sky, the fighting slowed – a few sporadic shots rattled around the valley like a coin in a tin can. Dad appeared at the door, and I shook off my sleepy haze. We ran out to the courtyard, where I took a deep sniff of air that smelled of gunpowder and the surrounding decomposition.

Outside and off-leash, I inhaled a bowl of kibble and then ran around to check in with the pack – they were still alert but starting to relax, eating dinner out of plastic bags and telling stories. I collected all leftovers, including some tasty cheese crackers from the Candy man, and then I humped a few blankets. It was a nice recess from the game stress, but the radio chirps warned us to start preparing for round two.

The sunlight faded and the pops started up again, followed by a rumbling just outside the compound walls. Dad returned me to the room where the air was as hot as my breath – and from there I listened to our opponents attack, and us respond with twice the force. As the night wore on, Dad came in during his recesses to sit and stretch his legs on a floor mat next to me, his head resting on his bag and his hand still on his gun. Together we slept until another member of the pack shook him awake to tag him back into the competition.

The game finally wound down the next afternoon, when our opponents grew quiet and seemed to run out of equipment. Dad took off some of his gear and scrubbed us both with a wet cloth; then he released me to explore the compound.

The pack was in high spirits, chatting and laughing as they piled up our trash and old game equipment. Meanwhile, I surveyed our opponents' residence, sniffing the oils on their clothes and mats – the kitchen odors were especially strong, with several layers of meat cauterized onto the metal stove.

Dad and I trotted over to a livestock pen that was attached to the compound, and he told me to "go potty." I ran around, sniffing hay and checking out the cows and goats that lived there. Their conditions made them unfriendly – the pen had very little shade or water, and the residents looked like skeletons draped in scarred, sun-bleached skin.

A large bull sauntered around the yard, huffing at me in disgust. As I lifted a leg to pee on a wooden post, he stared at my stream, accusing me of marking his turf. His thick hooves clomped towards me – deliberate and ready for confrontation – and his head turned downward as he threatened to slam me into the wall with his dense skull.

"*Bliven*," Dad said, and then muttered a string of curse words as he fixed his stance in front of me. He stood patiently as the bull charged, and lifted his foot out in front of him just seconds before contact – the bull crumpled into Dad's boot, stumbling backward in shock. He shook off the blow but conceded the pen, presenting us with his butt in a show of submission.

"Let's go," Dad said, rushing me back to the main compound. I was giddy about our victory, leaping around as Dad recounted the story to our team.

After the sun descended on the second day, the pack
scooped our equipment into bags and slung them
onto their backs – but they left the largest pile behind.
We began walking towards the mountains with quick
steps.

We were moving through a dark patch of desert when
the compound behind us exploded. It was a massive
fireball, but I was the only one who was startled – the
rest of the pack kept moving forward. Our opponents
resumed the tournament, lobbing pops and thuds
into the inferno that was now a good distance behind
us. I heard the whistle of the helicopters; and as
their swirling blades drew close, the rocks stung us
like angry bees. Dad and I were the last to hop into
the helicopter before it rose up away from the earth,

leaving our opponents to fight our ghosts.

We arrived back at the airfield, and after a short bus
ride to camp, Dad and I left the pack and shuffled to
our room. Dad stacked our game gear in the corner
and then heaped a pile of dinner into my bowl while I
drooled. I ate as Dad wiped the sticky dust off me; he
made piles while I dozed on our bunk.

Next thing I knew, my eyes cracked open at the click
of the door latch; Dad entered with food on his breath
and an armload of new supplies. We endured a stroll
just before dawn – Dad reminding me to "go potty"
with every step – before collapsing onto our bunk
and falling into fitful sleep, practicing for upcoming
competitions in our dreams.

****

Two nights later, I whined along with the helicopters that were coming to pick us up for the next game. The pack had spent that afternoon talking intently around a table and making their piles, and now we were lying on the gravel airfield looking up at the stars. My insides were churning in anticipation of what the night's games would bring.

The pack crowded into the helicopters that floated up into the night sky and swept over the shadowy landscape; they landed on rocky terrain and allowed us only a moment to hop off before they escaped. We began cutting a path through a marijuana field, the plants towering above our heads. Trampling through their wake of tangy scent, I snapped at the long leaves – they were surprisingly tasty.

"*Fooey! Hey, fooey!*" Dad whispered as I chewed.

We emerged from the field, and Dad gave me a "*sook!*" as we crept towards a set of buildings. The night was eerily silent, like everything had been frightened just a moment before. After I confirmed there were no bombs around the first building, the pack's terp announced the game rules and demanded our opponents come out. There was a pause, and then only the crickets responded.

"Find em!" Dad said as he swung open the large wooden door. I ran inside, searching the rooms for hidden opponents – and in the third room, I found one.

Without a shred of noise or light, my nose led me to human odor concentrated in the back corner. I padded carefully across the floor mats until my nose bumped a rubbery form that didn't react. The smell of decay, like browning spinach leaves, made me hesitate.

"Turbo, *here!*" Dad said just before I took a bite. I ran towards the sound of his voice as he shined a light on the old man sitting on a floor mat.

The old man's eyes did not move – his head followed his ears, so I knew he was blind. Dad leaned down and frisked his frail body. Finding nothing, he brought in the terp; and after a hoarse exchange, he reported that the man had been left here to die. The pack carefully secured his hands, pulled some papers from his pockets, and carried him out to the courtyard to sit while we completed our search.

According to the radios and hushed conferences within the pack, our opponents were hiding nearby. We regrouped in the courtyard to plan our next move when suddenly the game started – booms pounded the ground nearby, advancing towards us like the footsteps of an invisible giant. The pack dispersed, taking cover and installing equipment around the building. Our guns roared in retaliation.

Dad ushered the old man and me into a room. As he secured my leash to a wooden cabinet, an explosion hit so hard that the dirt on the floor jumped to head level, and everything was momentarily suspended in mid-air. My ears collapsed, and Dad cupped his hands over them before the next big thud jarred our intestines.

"You okay buddy?" he asked, then muttered, "Those danger close airstrikes have got to be messing up your ears."

Dad cuffed the old man to a post and told him not to move; then he ran back out to assist the pack. A couple of hours of pops and whooshes passed before the game slowed to a stop; the room became quiet, except for the ringing in my ears.

Dad came in and freed me to resume the competition. The radios were animated as we headed toward the far west corner of the village. The pack followed as I *sooked* a path towards a building ahead, with smoke billowing from its jagged walls; the smell of cremation hung in the air.

We entered the compound vigilant, scanning with our guns and noses. Charred limbs were lying around on the ground like puzzle pieces; the pack began collecting our opponents' guns and equipment from disconnected hands.

"*Sook!*" Dad hissed. I darted around, distracted by the ambient smell of explosives, and was finally drawn to an odor behind a wall curtain. Dad recalled me before my butt could hit the ground, and gave me a tennis ball to chew while our packmates drew back the curtain to reveal several large bags of bombs tucked into a wall cutout.

Once again, distant pops were followed by thuds landing nearby. We began our drill, claiming this compound as ours and setting up gun stations. Packmates attached white blocks to the adobe walls and connected them to wires; then Dad cupped his hands over my ears and the block exploded, leaving a porthole in the wall where our guns could peek out to fire at our opposition.

Dad escorted the old prisoner and me to another stuffy room – this one filled with mangled bodies and the smell of burnt hair. Dad tied me to a wooden post and told me to "*bliven*" before rushing back outside. Amidst the thunder of guns, my ears perked at the shriek of helicopters, and my tail began to thump.

The booms and radio traffic lasted several hours while the old man and I endured the stagnant air, and the smell of innards. Dad finally returned and we rejoined our pack, while the old man stayed back with the body parts. Dad had me *sook* the compound, but our opponents had taken their gear with them when they left.

We patrolled out of the village. I ran ahead, the pack following me under the weight of their huge packs. We charged down a long slope into a clearing where the cool night air spread out across the flat desert. My tail celebrated the sound of helicopters on the horizon; they touched down just long enough for everyone to hop in, and we were whisked back to the tarmac.

As we found our seats on the bus, the buzz was wearing off and I felt the soreness creeping into my muscles. We pulled up to camp and I tripped down the steps, wandering towards our room and the promise of cold air. I devoured a meal and curled up on the bunk, watching Dad organize our game gear. I tried to stay awake for his return from breakfast – but my eyelids surrendered to a long, dreamless slumber.

****

Two weeks into our deployment I was exhausted. My legs ached from the long insert hikes getting to the tournaments, and my pads were dry and cracked from the dry terrain. I treasured our break days, when Dad and I would wake in the afternoon, stretch, eat a meal and walk around camp; then we would return to our room for a nap, the cool air falling on us from above like snowflakes.

One afternoon, in between game days, I woke
when Dad returned from dinner carrying stacks
of equipment. His wet hair smelled like soap; it
reminded me of San Diego. I lounged in the bunk
while he cleaned his gun and arranged his piles,
jumping down every few minutes to place my ball
on top of his gear and propose a game of catch; Dad
would toss it up on the bunk, where I pounced on it
and settled in for a chew.

When the gear was ready for our next event, we
watched a movie and snacked on treats from Mom's
care packages, which Dad shared with visiting
packmates. Just before dawn we ate one last meal and
took a walk, returning to our bunk to sleep just as the
daylight began to infiltrate the room's cracks.

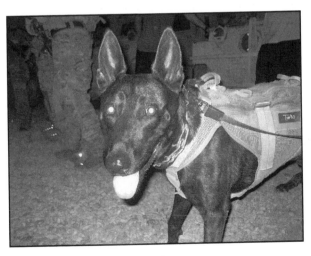

The next night, the helicopters came to pick us up right after sunset, and we landed in a flat sandy area surrounded by mountain peaks, bright under the rising full moon. I led the patrol up a rocky path *sooking* for bombs. When I found an odor, I pulled Dad towards it hard for a few steps – and then he would call me back to him.

"Thaaat's a good boy," he leaned down and whispered in my ear, rubbing my head.

Rather than locating the source, our entire crew changed direction, and I would lead us down the new route with my nose.

We walked to the base of a mountain; I tried to pull Dad sideways and around, but he directed me upwards. We started scaling rocks and hopping through shrub beds. When we were confronted with cliff walls, Dad helped me belly-crawl up the steep faces; I could smell the pack's odor rising up behind me. Just before the top of the ridge we paused to catch our breaths, and Dad broke out water and snacks.

The way down was just as sheer as the way up, so Dad spent a lot of time lowering me by my vest. When my feet touched the ground, he told me to *"bliven"* until he joined me down on the ledge. Finally I was able to *sook* the rest of the way on a switchback that led us to a fallow field; and we made our way over to a winding road bordered by trees.

As soon as I set foot on the road I smelled explosives and followed my nose towards a mound of dirt. Dad called me back before I could get close, and the pack inspected mound; then we took a long detour around to the backside of a cluster of structures.

Dad and I sniffed the village perimeter and found no bombs. The pack's terp told anyone inside that did not want to play should leave now; and we waited, but no one exited. Then the pack separated into two teams, and Dad guided me up to a large open door.

"*Find em!*" I ran in with the pack close behind. My nose prodded every nook and crevice for living odor, but our opponents had already evacuated.

I returned to Dad with no scores to report, and he ordered me to *sook*. I circled through the courtyard, making note of some goat poops I would eat later, and entered a room covered in floormats. My nose was immediately attracted to a wooden cabinet with faint odors leaking from the right side. I tried to find the source, scanning the panels and jumping to the top, and I finally ended up sitting next to the back right corner.

Dad gave me my tennis ball and a "good boy!" while another member of the pack investigated the cabinet, opening every compartment and emptying the contents. He tugged it away from the wall to look at its backside. Then he shrugged.

"Nope, man, nothing here," he said to Dad. "Just a bunch of fancy china.

Dad shook his head. "There's something in there. Turbo wouldn't sit on it if there wasn't. Check that back right corner again."

Our packmate dragged the cabinet further from the wall and knocked on the right side – a low, hollow thud – then on the left – a solid rap. He flattened his hand against the right side panel and slid it to the left, uncovering guns, explosives, and tennis ball-shaped grenades.

The pack collected the equipment while Dad and I *sooked* the rest of the compound. I explored two empty rooms and passed some tasty kitchen smells before entering a small pantry. My butt hit the floor when I smelled sharp ammonia odor emanating from a stack of bags piled against the back wall. Dad pulled me out of the room and handed me a ball while the pack's investigator checked the area, stabbing the sacks with his pocketknife. The top four bags contained flour, but explosive powder spilled out of the bottom two.

We continued searching the compound, and in the

center of the village I entered a building that smelled like yeast. My nostrils were caked with dust, but I detected an odor of live opponents, and followed it to a curtain hanging on the wall. I couldn't see anyone, but I ducked behind it to find a panel that smelled of human musk.

I barked at the drape and Dad ran in, giving me a thump on my chest. He pulled the curtain back with his gun ready, revealing the small wooden door.

"Hey, who cleared this room?" Dad asked the other pack members.

A young teammate across the hall yelled back, "I did."

"Did you check this door behind the curtain?" Dad asked.

"What door?"

Our packmate entered the room and pointed his gun at the wooden panel while Dad turned around and mule-kicked it open. We heard a cry come from the space inside, and then a weapon slid out. Dad and other packmates aimed their guns on the cubby as an opponent emerged, offering his empty hands in surrender. Dad pulled him out and frisked him for equipment before tying his hands behind his back.

We continued working our way through the village,

and I found a few more bomb stashes before shots rang out, disrupting our search. We heard the rustle of waking villagers just as the pack's radios started buzzing about some "squirters" that had challenged us to a match.

Dad and I were selected to join a small team to compete against the "squirters." We scurried to the southern end of the village, down to a road that ran parallel to a river corridor. Large trees lining the right side of the road concealed the water from view; to the left, low-lying crops led up to a fruit orchard.

With the leash attached to my vest, Dad whispered, "*find em*." I had only taken a few steps before I found a skunky odor and pulled hard into the wind, charging into the muddy riverbank after the target – but Dad tugged me back to him, praising me as we ran back up the road.

"Yah, *braffy*, I know you found them. Don't worry – we won't let them get away."

The pack crouched behind a short retaining wall with a view of the riverbed. Dad whispered, "*aufliggen*," and pushed my back to the ground as the pack lined up with their guns propped on the wall. Once in place, the terp announced to our opponents that they must surrender in order to avoid death. The declaration was followed by a silent beat, and then the crickets resumed their songs as our pack listened for a stir.

I was the first to hear legs struggling through the thick river underbrush – one of our opponents popped out into the moonlight, gun in hand, and sprinted across the field towards the orchard. As I watched him approach the goal line under the trees, I pleaded with Dad to be released so I could make the tackle; but Dad's goggles were tracking the figure, and his gun discharged twice. Our adversary faltered – he staggered the short distance to the tree line and vanished from sight.

The terp made more announcements in the direction of the river, and seven opponents surfaced, forfeiting the match. They handed over their weapons and we cuffed them, forcing them to lie on their bellies in the grass while the pack stood guard.

Dad and I walked over to the orchard where the squirter had run. The terp shouted announcements under the tree canopy, but there was no response. Dad unclipped my leash.

"Find em."

I followed the scent of blood that led me to the body; I nudged his cooling skin, but the opponent didn't react. I stood guard until the pack arrived.

We ran back to the compound and united with the

rest of our crew, which started hiking a south-trending path with our seven river prisoners and one cubbyhole opponent in tow. We made it to a field where we lingered a moment, listening to the birds and bugs around us; then I heard the purr of our helicopters. They crested over the horizon of a nearby ridgeline, coming to settle in front of us on the field.

The crowded ride to camp was short, and when we arrived, the opponents were loaded into vans with blindfolds covering their eyes; I never saw them again. Our pack returned to camp to fill our bellies and rest up before the next event.

****

Dad and I took daily potty walks around camp, and sometimes we stopped at a long building where the rest of the pack lived. The main door led to a hallway with a row of rooms along one side – I ran in to calls of "Turbo!" and received head-pats and chest-thumps as I shimmied down the narrow passage, nosing through bags and bunks – there was always plenty of food and toys low to the ground. Dad tried his best to prevent me from eating the pack's discards, but extra snacks were always worth a *"fooey."*

Some nights when we had no events scheduled, the pack gathered around the glow of a fire to banter and squawk like a bunch of ravens. Packmates took turns calling me over to give me rough pets and dust-covered treats from their pockets, as others told stories with their entire bodies, casting monstrous shadows onto the desert floor. These nighttime parties were more fun than our indoor afternoon planning sessions, where I was always getting a *"fooey"* and a *"leave it!"* for sifting through the trashcans.

Our pack was a brotherhood; we had played many matches together, and we rooted for each other's victories. After one of our more taxing hikes to a village deep in the desert one night, we had searched so many buildings that my tongue was coated in a thick dirt paste. My joints ached, and my vest chafed my neck and armpits. The wisps of mid-August breeze weren't cool enough to provide any relief.

It had been an uneventful night, so the pack decided to throw a quick party for Dad and some other mates who had "made rank." Our pack leader read a proclamation and pinned a little gold anchor to Dad's collar.

Candy man stood beside me, rubbing my head. "So if you are a Chief, that makes Turbo a Senior Chief," he said. Then he leaned down and smacked my side with a laugh. "Hooyah, Senior Chief Turbo!"

Dad smiled under his beard. Then we went back to searching buildings; the party was over.

It was just before dawn, the black sky fading to violet; and we walked through the desert at a fast clip that told me we were headed back to camp. My ears scanned for the pick-up helicopters, which held the promise of dinner and a cool bunk.

The stars were dimming as I crested a small hill *sooking* for bombs, and a breeze rushed up the other side carrying the smell of rot. I took a few more steps over the ridge and he came into view – a big Anatolian Shepherd, mad with hunger.

Our eyes locked and we froze, sizing each other up. His body was scarred, and his eyes vacant within his hollow face – there was no soul inside. I was healthier and better trained, but desperation gave him an advantage. He snarled, and I responded with a growl.

Starving, he took his chance on offense, stalking up the path on a damaged hind leg. I stood, still and ready, preparing to strike the right side of his neck. He drew near, surrounded by a cloud of disease – and just as I was about to vault forward, a roar of blasts erupted behind me. My enemy vanished; there was nothing left but a veil of red mist hanging in the air.

I swung around to see Dad and the pack standing behind me, their guns pointed at the spot where the dog had been a moment before. I sniffed the fog of blood and found traces of his disease.

I ran up to Dad, but he was not in the mood to celebrate; we hurried to the helicopters that took us back to camp.

We had received no points for making the dog disappear, but we seemed to be winning the game. Our crew had amassed a huge stockpile of our opponents' game equipment. None of our packmates had been hurt, and we had killed off packs several times our size; but our opponents seemed to have an infinite supply of players, so the games continued.

Our perfect record came to an end in our third month of deployment. The pace of the tournament had not slowed, but I couldn't say the same about my body. After Dad dressed us in our gear one game day, I curled up on the bed to remind him how comfortable it was.

He smiled. "I know you'd rather stay, but we have an op tonight. Put on your game face."

Dad and I met the pack at the fire barrel, and we all loaded onto the buses for a ride to the baked hardscape of the airfield. When the helicopters arrived, whipping us with rocks and promising a bumpy ride, I looked up at Dad and whined, "*Are you sure you want to go?*"

We stepped off the bird into a dust storm to begin the night's event. The pack tried to get its bearings within the haze of dirt, taking a few steps forward and colliding into a clay wall. The pack exchanged hushed words, and the village buzzed, awakened by the sound of our helicopters.

Even when our visibility increased, the pack seemed frustrated, but we fell into formation. Dad had me *sook* the perimeter of the buildings – I came back with nothing – and the terp made his usual announcements, but no opposing players emerged. Dad sent me in to look for humans; finding none, he instructed me to *sook*. There were no explosive stashes to report, but the pack seized a stack of papers and electronic equipment.

After a conference and a great deal of pointing, the

pack split up – our team hustled southwest towards a small, brushy hilltop, while the other unit moved north towards a broad, path-worn mountain.

I darted up the rocky path, *sooking* through thorny bushes and weeds. Our team gathered at the peak overlooking a line of garages called a "bazaar," and I confirmed that there were no traps in the area. Then our crew started building a nest of sand bags at the summit while I wandered the perimeter looking for rabbit droppings.

Construction of the perch was completed and four of our packmates got inside, pointing their guns down at the bazaar below. Once they were in position, the rest of us began a careful trek down the hill's steep path; I led the way, searching for bombs, with Dad and a few packmates following in my footsteps.

We were about halfway down the hill when an explosion rocked the mountain next to us, where the other half of our team had gone to climb. A huge fireball lit up the sky, fading into a dark puff of smoke that blotted out the stars. The land around us went silent, as though tensing for an aftershock.

Our team stood fixed behind me, staring at the mountain – the other half of our pack somewhere on it – quietly cursing, "*Oh shit…*"

I tried to ignore the ringing in my ears as I listened for noise from the blast site. Then a breeze passed by with odors of blood and cinnamon, and I knew our teammate Stan had been hurt. He was one of the pack's leaders – kind, smart, and a great athlete. Our opponents had scored their first victory.

Ants bit my ankles as we stood watching the smoke and shadows hover over the mountain. An uneasy quiet was interrupted by the radio crackling to life – Stan had stepped on a hidden bomb. He'd been wounded – his legs were gone.

There was pain in the radio voice, and the pack's energy was sapped by the words. Some cursed our opponents as we sat with heavy spirits, listening to calm and urgent tones take turns on the radio.

After some discussion, a few members of our crew ran off to assist Stan, while the remainder of our team pushed forward. We trudged down the hill, our jaws stiff with anger, eyes flashing over to the smoldering mountain. The packs' guns were on high alert. Minutes later, a helicopter zipped in and landed, off-loading several people who lifted Stan into the machine and flew him away.

At the bottom of the hill, Dad removed my leash so I could *sook* the bazaar. Sniffing the ground and walls, I found hints of bread, tea, spices, cloth, and wood,

but nothing worthy of a tennis ball. At the far end of
the marketplace we came to a fork in the road, where
I detected a bomb covered by a pile of dirt. Before I
could sit Dad called me over for a ball, and I chewed
it like a wad of gum as our investigators examined
the mound and carefully stacked white bricks on top.
They twisted a plastic piece and the mound exploded –
chunks of earth shot high into the sky.

Just then, as if triggered by our blast, a series of
pops and crashes erupted in the village behind us.
Our packmates responded with a roar of firepower
from their hilltop perch, and suddenly bombs were
screaming over our heads as Dad and I ducked
behind one of the booths. From there we listened
to the whoosh of jets, followed by huge explosions;
Dad covered my ears with his hands, leaving his own
exposed.

The ruckus lasted over an hour, and finally tapered off
at dawn. Dad tied my long leash to a tree so he could
meet with the rest of the pack, and I stretched out
in the dirt and surveyed the barren land around me,
dotted with white stones and a few gnarly trees. Under
a nearby bramble, the morning light had revealed a
family of rabbits casually nibbling on a patch of green
sprouts. They were unfazed by my presence – even
when I stood up, they looked right at me and continued
eating. One of them taunted me with his quick
movements, as if to imply that he was faster than me.

After several minutes of watching them hop around with impunity, I bolted toward them. I could hear Dad yelling my name in the background. *"Not now, Dad..."* I thought. *"I have to teach these bunnies a lesson."*

I didn't notice the whir of my leash until I heard it hit the end of its slack. The collar wrenched my neck against my own momentum – I did a full backflip and hit the ground with a thud.

I shook off the dirt as I got back on my feet, realizing I had just given myself a very hard correction. Walking slowly back to my disturbed spot by the tree, I cursed those filthy rabbits and their trickery.

Dad jogged over, shaking his head. "Well, you kicked your own ass that time," he said, looking at my neck.

Once he confirmed I had not done any damage, he unclipped my leash.

We ran back to the fork in the road where we had blown up my earlier find. Dad directed me to "sook," and I made my way down to a set of sheds at the end of the path, sniffing around the exterior walls. Once I gave him the all clear, Dad mule-kicked each of the rusty shed doors open, revealing inky-dark space inside. As our team held their guns ready, Dad sent me into each of the structures to search for humans and bombs.

I quickly advanced to the last shed – I knew it would be a winner. My nose led me to the center of the room, where it reeked of explosives, but I couldn't find a source. I circled the interior and sniffed the floor where the scent was most intense, and finally I sat and waited for my reward.

Dad's flashlight found me, and I heard him say, "Turbo, *here!*" I bounded out to him, and he tossed me a ball as our packmates opened a hatch on the floor. Inside, they found so many bags of ammonium nitrate and aluminum powder that we couldn't carry them all home. The team placed a pile of white blocks in the center of the shed and attached it to a long wire; then we all ran to the other end of the bazaar and hunkered down behind a concrete wall. Dad covered me with his entire body.

When the shed blew, the blast was so intense my brain vibrated – I was nauseous and dazed, scanning the wide eyes of teammates who appeared equally stunned. Dad whispered "holy shit" under his breath, and we watched a dark orange cloud build above our heads.

We patrolled south and met up with the rest of our pack – all of us moved quickly down a hill, through a fig orchard, and out to a clearing. Nature was slowly recovering from our last explosion – the hum of bugs, followed by a wave of bird chirps. My pulse picked up when I heard helicopters in the distance, and I strained against my leash to meet them; my tail waved them into the landing zone.

"Yeah, you can tell he likes the sound of those extract helos," Dad murmured to a friend as I hopped aboard – one step closer to our air-conditioned room back at camp.

****

The competition intensified after Stan's injury – our opponents were planting bombs everywhere to take out more of our players. I was happy to rack up points finding their hidden traps, but I could feel Dad's blood pressure rise as we made our way through the game fields. I pulled him towards several winning odors, but before I could score a ball he would redirect our platoon to a new path, ordering them to walk precisely in our tracks and sending me out for another "sook." He was not in the mood to play.

One evening, the helicopter dropped us off at the starting point of a long sook event. After several odor detections and redirects, we hiked through a watermelon patch to a well-worn road. Dad unhooked my leash and commanded me to sook along a short wall bordering one side of the path. I dashed ahead, surveying odors of animal dung and trash, but finding no bombs.

The path sloped downwards and I followed it to the wall's end, where I made a quick turn – and walked right into an ambush. Staring back at me were two Anatolian Shepherds, tall and gaunt, creeping towards me with low, raspy growls. I squared off to them and readied for battle – I would aim my first bite at the front one's right leg, snapping it before the smaller dog was in range to strike. Then I would pin the small one by the throat, daring the injured one to re-attack.

As they drew close, I could smell the rotten organs on their breath. Hunkering down, I bared my teeth and snarled – *bring it on.*

Suddenly, they froze. Their eyes widened – they seemed to be looking at a spirit hovering just above me. Then their legs shifted into reverse, tail tucked, and I watched them accelerate in a full retreat. They had sensed that I was fearless and realized they were not up to the match.

I turned around to see my entire pack standing behind me, their guns pointed over my head. I ran up to Dad, my tail wagging. *"Did you see that?"* I asked, searching his face.

"Yeah, *braffy,"* Dad laughed. "You scared the shit out of those boys! That was all you." He gave me a head rub.

The rest of the pack laughed too, as I ran around collecting proud chest thumps.

"Nice work, Senior Chief!"

"Turbo was about to kick some ass!"

Three nights later, Dad had his own face-off. There was an October chill in the air as our helicopters landed on the southern edge of a marijuana field. We hopped off and I began patrolling through the rows of plants, *sooking* the dry earth for hidden bombs. The tall stalks hid the half-moon, and I snapped at leaves that brushed against my face in the dark.

Our radios were active, and their transmissions were heightening the pack's tension. We emerged from the field and turned onto a narrow path, lined by hemp on one side and a tree-lined river canal on the other. Dad ordered me to *sook* and I sniffed for patterns, crossing back and forth between the base of the crops and the water's edge – but the only breaths of wind were coming from behind me, carrying the scents of our pack.

As I drifted into a curve in the road, the leash pulled to the end of its range, so I stopped and trotted back to Dad. My eyes searched the shadows to make out his form – he was crouching to see under the trees, his attention on something down the road in front of us. Then he stood and took a few steps forward. I could see the outline of his aggressive stance, and the gun extending from his nose.

"*Lasuna portica!*" Dad shouted.

It was a command so powerful that the world around us went mute. I was stunned, desperate to comply, but I didn't recognize the words.

133

Then I heard stirring behind me and I turned to see a figure. A dress glowed in the moonlight. I sniffed the air for information but the wind only smelled like Dad.

The man in the dress was still for a moment; his head turned slightly as he tried to locate Dad's voice in the shadows. Finding nothing, his hands slowly began rising into the air, reaching just above his shoulders before he paused. Suddenly his hands changed course, moving back down towards his waist. His left hand slipped under the fold of his clothes and pulled out a long, shiny gun.

Three blasts cracked over my head, and a sharp burst of gunpowder saturated the air. The enemy's knees buckled, and he crumpled to the ground. His hand continued moving, threatening a response, but a final shot blew out the back of his head.

I ran up, sniffing the sweetness that seeped out of his wounds. Dad stalked up behind me, his gun still ready in case our opponent had his own pack in tow. He glanced down and kicked a gun out of our opponent's hand; then he bent down to check the eyelids for death. There was no movement – no one left inside.

Dad stood, his eyes and gun fixed on the dark path ahead. One of our packmates came up to inspect the dead opponent, pulling his robes back to reveal a second gun and a radio.

Dad's eyes glanced down at the body as he hissed into his radio, "One enemy KIA carrying two AK-47s and a radio. Someone in the back of the patrol pick this shit up – we're leaving it next to the body."

We continued forward, *sooking* our way to a large compound where the pack collected for a muffled conference. Dad had me sniff the walls, and I returned with no finds; then he gave our terp a nod to begin the announcements. Women and children filtered out of the building with bleary eyes, stumbling to an area where they would be guarded by our pack. We searched the building for bites and bombs, but there were no targets inside.

The pack remained vigilant as we received radio messages about opponents on the move. We jogged to a second compound, where I sniffed and the terp called out the rules to no response. Dad pulled open the wooden door and gave me a *"find em"* command, and I sprinted inside. I found no opponents in the first three rooms – only floor mats that smelled like their butts.

Then I came upon a set of stairs that led to the roof. I ran up and sniffed to the edge, stopping to scan the mountain ridge on the horizon before turning and running to the other end, where I jumped down to a lower roof platform on my left. I ran along that roofline to the back of the building – beneath me I could smell the sleeping quarters. Again I walked to the end and jumped down – realizing one second too late that the next landing was the ground, far below.

I hit the hard dirt of the courtyard – my right wrist took the brunt of the impact and recoiled. I rolled to my side, my arm exploding with pain, and I yelped for Dad.

Candy man ran to me and helped me struggle upright, holding my paw off the ground. Then Dad appeared – his stance defensive – ready to fight. His shoulders dropped when he saw me on the ground, and he fell to his knees, checking me for injuries.

"What happened?" Dad asked. "Is he okay? Did he get attacked?"

Candy man shrugged. "I don't know, man. All I saw was him leaping off the roof."

Dad shook his head and groaned, "*br-r-raffy*," as he inspected my legs. When he touched my wrist I whined – *Yep, that's it. That's the one.*

Dad helped me to a room and onto a floor mat, instructing me to "*aufliggen*" and "*bliven*." He attached my leash to a post and ran out to rejoin the pack.

I lay still, nibbling at my aching wrist. When the familiar hailstorm of pops and explosions began, I knew the pack was hustling, setting up on the corners of the roof and fashioning nests made of sandbags. Dad checked on me every so often, at one point shooting a needle of medicine into my arm. Then I slept, the pain distant.

The volleys continued through the night and into the dawn – a blur of cracks and crashes, answered by heavy blasts. I stirred when it shook the walls, and relaxed when I heard the hum of air support.

By mid-afternoon, the blasts subsided and silence settled over the region. Dad came in and checked my legs before propping himself up next to me for a quick doze. I rested my head on his leg and relaxed into a peaceful sleep. It seemed like only a moment later when a packmate woke Dad for an event and then stole his nap spot.

Several hours passed in that toasty room, as I listened to occasional pops and blasts, the pack shouting directions, and the thump of rocket launchers in the courtyard. Then the quiet would set in, and pack members would come to pick out a spot among the floor mats, sleeping in shifts.

When night returned, the pack began sorting trash and equipment into piles. Dad gave me a shot before we patrolled out, masking the pain as I limped to the landing zone on three legs. Dad rooted me on – "just a little farther!" – and every so often he asked, "You doing okay, buddy?"

The helicopters finally swooped down, and he lifted me inside.

"We're almost there."

Had I known that getting hurt would give me a break from the games, I might have jumped off a roof sooner – but had I known that Dad was going to keep playing without me, I would have suppressed that first painful yelp.

****

Back in our room I laid on the bunk, my arm taped up to the elbow, watching Dad put on his game gear. My vest dangled on its hook.

As he loaded up his equipment and weapon, and heaved the huge bag onto his back, he couldn't even look at me. I jumped out of the bunk onto my three good legs, staring up at my game vest on the hook.

Dad shook his head. "No *braffy*. You're not going tonight."

He patted the bunk and gave me a "*hoog*." I jumped up and wobbled through two circles into a curl. Dad rubbed between my ears and scratched under my chin.

"You stay here and rest," he said before he left. The door latched, footsteps, and then he was gone. Out there, by himself.

I spent the next several hours trying to sleep, waking at the slightest noise – the buzz of the air unit, vehicles driving in the distance, the camp's loudspeaker. Every time I heard motion in the hallway I held my breath, watching the doorknob.

In the morning, I was ripped out of a dream by the jiggle of the door handle – I leapt off the bed, still asleep, not thinking about my arm until it hit the floor with a shock of pain.

Dad's friend entered with a cheerful, "Hey Turbo!"

I sniffed his clothes – there was no Dad on them. He poured me a bowl of kibble topped with pills, and we became friends. For about an hour, he talked and played on a computer while I watched the door. Then we went on a painful walk around camp. I did my business, searched for tennis balls, and ran towards every man that could be Dad.

We returned to the room but my friend did not stay, and he closed the door behind him. I slept through most of the day, still listening for the door latch. As the hours passed, I started to worry – *what if he never came back...*

I was disappointed when Dad's friend reappeared, my wagging tail slowing to a droop. He fed me and we went on another walk under stars just blinking to life in the darkening sky. Dad's scent was nowhere to be found.

I limped back to the room and hopped up on the bunk. "Your Dad will be back soon," our friend said as he left.

I nestled under the string of tube lights in the haze of my painkillers, and woke the next morning to the roar of the cold air unit doing battle with the morning sun. I heard the swishes of jets on the airfield. Then there was a shuffling at the door – the smell of Dad entered before he did.

"Hey buddy! Hey *braffy!*" he squealed as I leapt off the bed to tackle him. "Did you miss me?" His face was exhausted but happy – I licked a clean spot into the coating of dirt.

He scrubbed my head and went to remove his gear as I celebrated, knocking my hurt leg into walls. Dad laughed and gave me a chest thump with his palm. "Settle down, buddy. Calm down. I missed you too." I melted down the side of his leg.

"You want some breakfast?" Dad asked. I dusted the floor with my tail while he fixed me a bowl of kibble with a pill chaser. Then he vanished, reappearing later with a meal on his breath. After a quick tour of the camp, we returned to our room and squished into opposite ends of the bunk for a long nap.

Chapter 6

Trainer Ben

I spent a few more excruciating nights alone, waiting
for Dad to return from events – then one afternoon he
began making piles of gear and placing them in metal
travel boxes. On our walk that evening, his phone call
with Mom was upbeat. The next day, we swung by the
building where Hammer used to live and found Diesel
and his dad settling into the room. They had arrived to
take our spot in the competition – our deployment was
over.

We rose before the sun the next morning and boarded
the first of many planes, landing a couple of times to
stay in hotels along the way. We stopped in one balmy
city where green vines covered the buildings; then
another where the streets smelled like sausage and
beer. The next plane landed in America on a cold, gray
afternoon – I hobbled down the plane ramp to a patch
of soft, wet grass and begged Dad for a ball.

We boarded one final flight that touched down just
after sunset. The hatch opened and the smell of the
ocean let me know we were home – back in San Diego,
where the games were easy and we spent more time

playing catch than making piles. I bolted to the nearest pee post, while Dad gathered our game gear. Mom greeted us at the airport, squeezing us both. She smelled sweet, not a hint of goat.

We loaded the car with our Afghanistan-scented bags and drove north towards my favorite place in the world – the park. As we drew close I began a celebration of wobbly spins. Dad opened the door and I limped out to get a lungful of grass, sage, and rabbit pellets – my own welcome home party.

"What if he hurts himself?" Mom asked. She did not have a stomach for our games.

We arrived at Dad's house and I sprinted inside as fast as I could on three legs, ignoring the pain in my wrist. Dad laughed. "Someone is happy!"

I sniffed the carpet and the couch, and memories of San Diego life flooded back. Dad ate from a feast Mom had prepared, and she slipped me pieces of food under the table. Relief was in the air.

Later that night, Dad told me to "*hoog*," patting a fuzzy blanket on the couch; he helped me climb up and I curled into a ball. "Night-night *braffy*. We'll see you in the morning." Mom kissed my nose.

The house became dark, and I listened to the staircase creak from the back and forth of their footsteps.

"I can't believe you let him have the couch," Dad whispered.

"He is an injured combat vet. Of course he gets the couch," Mom said.

The house was silent except for a few muffled sounds upstairs. There were no helicopters whining, no explosions popping – not even any dogs barking. I felt like I slept for days.

****

I awoke the next morning on the couch and enjoyed a mild San Diego morning that started with kibble and a sunbath. The contrast with Afghanistan was extreme – life was suddenly peaceful and lazy. Dad and I did our best to unwind, to be casual like Mom, but I was worried about whether our opponents had followed us back to San Diego.

I did have one enemy to contend with at home – they called her The Cat. She was a little black creature that lived upstairs and had control over the entire floor. Based on her smell she was at least a hundred years old, but fast like a demon. After my unfortunate rabbit-chasing incident, I was trying to resist the urge to hunt – but The Cat paraded around her territory, taunting me, acting as though I was too dumb or lame to catch her.

We had been introduced at the base of the stairs. I wagged my tail – maybe a little overzealously – and she responded by smacking me in the face three times with her paw. I was stunned, but Dad pulled me away and told me to *"leave her."* From then on, he enforced an invisible force field of protection around her.

The Cat's dodgy maneuvers convinced me that she was hiding a treasure of food upstairs, but she governed that entire floor of the house, and was able to demand meal deliveries. Dad got angry when I cornered her behind the toilet one morning, lifting me backwards with an angry *"FOOEY!"* After that I decided she wasn't worth the hassle.

With the exception of The Cat's iron rule over the second floor, I loved home life – the soft couch, good food, and occasional trips to the park. But the deployment tournament haunted me. I was suspicious of movements in the shadows, always mentally prepared to do battle. I could tell Dad's mind was still on the game too, because his body never fully relaxed.

In the evening, Mom, Dad and I would stroll the neighborhood, checking out the local pee hubs. One chilly evening under a cloudless sky, Dad took me off leash to explore, and I went to find rabbit turds.

We were almost back to the house when I heard a rustling inside of a knotty bush. I sniffed, and tried to crawl underneath but sharp branches drove me back. Intrigued, I darted around the edges, pushing my nose inside until I saw moonlight shining off a pair of eyes…

It was the beady little eyes of The Cat.

Outside of Dad's protection, she was fair game. I chased her toward the side yard, eager to get a whiff of her butt to find out what kind of food she'd been hiding. She ducked under a fence into the next yard and I hurdled it, registering pain in my wrist as it hit the ground. We sprinted across the grass, crunching through fall leaves.

At the sound of my scampering feet, Dad yelled my

146

name. "Turbo, *here*!" I knew I only had a few more moments to catch her.

I finally cornered her against a wall, circling to get around to her backside. She glared at me, and it was the first time I noticed a bleached streak down her back... the Cat at home was solid black.

Regardless, I moved in for a sniff, and she surprised me by swinging around, tail erect. I closed in – and placed my face directly in a stream of her demon piss. Stunned by her immense power, I took a step back as she disappeared behind the toxic cloud; then I ran out to the street, my nose twitching from the burn.

"What's the matter? Did you run through a spiderweb?" Dad asked. He knelt down next to me, as the foul order spread out around us.

"He got sprayed by a skunk," Mom hissed.

She and Dad started scrambling. We all ran to the front door, but only Mom was allowed inside. Dad and I stood on the porch listening to her race up and down the stairs, lights turning on and off. She emerged with buckets full of a soap that Dad scrubbed into my fur. He blotted my face with Mom's brew, and then rinsed me with freezing water from the garden hose.

I shook and tried to bolt inside where it was warm, but Dad held me back. Mom brought out another bucket,

and Dad rubbed it in my coat. I shivered; and that
toxic butt spray was still in my eyes, making me sneeze.

After several cold baths, Dad and I were finally allowed
in the house, heading directly to the shower to sit in
the warm water. Dad dried me off with an old towel,
and Mom and Dad took turns *sooking* my head before
letting me jump onto the couch, which was covered in
layers of sheets and blankets. We were all exhausted –
they said goodnight and trudged upstairs.

After that night, Dad warned me to stay away from
those "black-and-white kitties" whenever he took me
off leash around our neighborhood; but I'd learned
my lesson. After getting a taste of the secret poison in
their butts, I no longer wanted a whiff.

****

My wrist healed, despite my best efforts to re-injure it
diving after tennis balls. No longer having an excuse
to be Mom's taste-tester, Dad and I returned to work to
find things had changed; we had new players living in
the kennel house.

Storm, Loki and Hammer were still there, joined by
two new residents named Speedy and Jazz. Speedy
was a dark Dutchie that lived in the kennel next to
mine; he was friendly one moment, testy the next. Jazz
was a blonde Belgian Malinois with a compact build

and a dark face, like he had dipped it in a bucket of
ink. Good-natured and talkative, Jazz loved training,
loved other dogs, and loved his new dad – all of this
enthusiasm irritated Loki to no end.

A few days later, a little brown Belgian named Ace
arrived. He was a sweet, empty-headed puppy with an
endless supply of energy. He spent his days digging
trenches and painting poop on walls; and then he
yapped about it all night long. Loki screamed at him
to shut up, and the two of them went back and forth for
hours. During recess and training, Ace was a spaz –
pouncing, nipping at fingers and faces, just begging for
a smack down.

Diesel was still away on deployment; and Trainer
Pete had vanished. The dads were interviewing new
trainers, and one sunny afternoon we met Trainer Ben.

The first time I saw him – a stocky man with worn
hands – he entered our kennel house alongside Dad.
"Let's do a bite evolution with one of the dogs and see
how it goes," Trainer Ben said in an easy voice.

The dads walked us all out to gather on the training
field. Trainer Ben crouched down in front of me, eyes
averted, and allowed me to sniff him; then he gave me
a chin scratch and stood up. After meeting all the dogs,
he walked over to our shed and returned wearing a
heavy, cushioned bite suit.

Trainer Ben waddled out to the middle of our training field. All of us dogs were giddy – my back legs were trembling – but the dads agreed to let Storm go first.

Still attached to his dad's leash, Storm was psyched for his first match against Trainer Ben. But instead of just waving his arms and stomping his feet, Trainer Ben actually seemed to get angry. He squared his shoulders to Storm, ready to fight. Storm started to whine. *"Are we sure the new guy knows how to play?"*

Released with a *"stellan,"* Storm sprinted down field, jumping to get a shallow bite of an outstretched forearm. Trainer Ben whipped Storm around, spinning him off his feet and moving with a quickness we had not seen before. They struggled for several minutes until Trainer Ben accepted defeat by growing still.

Storm was relieved to win the unusually tough bout. When his dad approached to choke him off the bite, Storm responded with his typical spin move to get away.

Trainer Ben held his free arm out at Storm's dad to stop him. "Tell him to *los,*"Trainer Ben instructed.

Storm's dad shook his head,"I have to choke him off. He doesn't have a verbal out. He won't respond to the *los* command."

"Sure he will,"Trainer Ben said waving him off. "Tell

him to *los*."

"*Los!*"

Storm became more anxious. To him, "*los*" meant "here comes the choke."

"Come over and pet him," Trainer Ben said. "Calm him down. Long, slow strokes. Then back away and give him the command again."

Storm and his dad were equally confused by this game, but his dad complied, and after some soothing pets, he repeated the "*los!*"

Storm hung on. Everyone looked at Trainer Ben.

"Now we wait," he said.

We waited a long time. Storm's feet dangled, his jaw most certainly ached; but Trainer Ben stood, fixed like a statue. Storm tried to get a foothold on Trainer Ben's hip, but Trainer Ben dodged Storm's legs, forcing him to hold his own weight.

Finally, feeling the slip in Storm's jaws, Trainer Ben instructed his dad, "As soon as you see him let go, you pair it with the *los* command. I'm going to immediately give him a re-bite as a reward."

Storm's teeth finally gave way and his dad called out,

"*los!*" before his feet hit the ground. Then there was a "*stellan*, as Trainer Ben tugged his arm back, like prey in retreat. Storm attacked while his dad encouraged him, "*that's a good boy!*" His tail wagged.

When it was time to "*los*" again, Storm's hang time was only slightly shorter than his first session, but he eventually let go. After a few rounds, Storm tried releasing as soon as he heard the "*los,*" and he quickly got another bite. Then his dad clipped a leash to his collar and Storm did a proud lap back to the car. It was a decisive victory.

From that day on, Trainer Ben directed our practices. His training events were intense – our bite work was more combative, but I knew from my deployment fight that our opponents were as well. Trainer Ben thrashed, rolled, kicked, and sweated; at the end of the event he was panting too. We were preparing for war.

Trainer Ben's courses were designed to teach us how to defeat a human, which is no simple task – humans are strong wrestlers, and very willing to kill an opponent in battle. He began by teaching us to target new areas of the body. Dad tied my leash to a tree, and then Trainer Ben positioned his puffy-suited leg just out of my reach. I snarled and leapt at it while the dads cheered. When I was finally released, I hit Trainer Ben's outstretched thigh, and he writhed and yelped in submission. We practiced targeting a calf, butt, knee, even the head. It was a revelation that opened up several new bite angles.

Some of the dogs hated the new changes to our training regimen. Loki didn't like Trainer Ben – the two of them engaged in long, stubborn matches that left him exhausted. Hammer disagreed with the new game rules, and refused to bite legs; arms were the traditional – and most effective – path to victory according to Hammer.

But Trainer Ben proved him wrong. Next bite practice, Hammer was released with a "*stellan*" and sprinted down the field at Trainer Ben. As he jumped, Trainer Ben raised his leg out in front of him, and Hammer collided with his foot mid-leap – he dropped to the ground, stunned. He turned to re-attack, but Trainer Ben punted him away every time. Frustrated, Hammer finally bit the outstretched leg, and received a roar of "good boys!" from the dad gallery. Trainer Ben made a great show of defeat.

Then Trainer Ben added a new rule that required dogs to be silent before starting their event – a rule that was strictly enforced when we played in Afghanistan. I had never been much of a talker so it didn't affect me, but the adjustment was hard for Loki and Hammer, whose dads had encouraged them to talk shit before a bite match.

The first day that the no-barking rule was imposed, the sight of a padded Trainer Ben walking onto the field sparked Loki's rage. "*Let me at him!*" he screamed, straining against the leash. His dad responded with a stern "*fooey*," and Trainer Ben took several steps further out of Loki's range. Loki continued his tizzy, drawing more "*fooeys*" from his dad, and Trainer Ben kept moving further down field until he was almost out of sight. When Loki stopped to catch his breath, Trainer Ben took a few steps closer. Then Loki barked and Trainer Ben retreated.

The dance went on like this for a while until a tense silence was reached, seconds slowly turning into minutes. The whisper of a whine threatened to end the unspoken treaty, but Loki finally lured Trainer Ben into bite range, and his dad unclipped him with an excited "*stellan!*" Loki wrestled Trainer Ben into submission to great fanfare from the dads.

Over the next few months, Trainer Ben revealed many of our opponents' tactics and taught us how to respond. During one bite practice, Dad gave me a "*stellan*" and I shot forward at a puffy-suited Trainer Ben, my ears folded back for speed. I jumped with about four strides between us, targeting his right shoulder. He stood, looking me in the eyes – and then his body turned – and I flew right past him.

I hit the ground and shook off my surprise, charging

back at him like a raging bull. I launched and
whiffed again, and then again, each time getting more
frustrated. Trainer Ben taunted me as I buzzed past
him, a smirk creeping across his face.

My legs grew tired, and I stopped to catch my breath.
Finally, I planned an attack targeting his lower body,
which would give me time to change course when
he shifted to one side. I sprinted at him, taking three
more strides than normal. When Trainer Ben's body
twisted, I tacked right along with it. *I've got you now* – I
growled.

I sprung and hit his leg hard, getting a mouthful
of inner thigh near his groin; I could feel his heart
pumping against my teeth. He let out a little squeak,
and his smile changed to a wince.

"Good boy! Yaah, *braffy!*" Dad and the others cheered.

I thrashed back and forth and Trainer Ben quickly
surrendered, signaling Dad to give me the "*los!*" We
did a few more run-throughs, and I practiced watching
his center mass for signs of a dodge.

After the final "*los,*" Dad clipped on my leash. Trainer
Ben chuckled. "He definitely has that one down – can't
juke that dog anymore!" he said, rubbing the soreness
out of his leg. Now I was the one wearing a smirk.

****

Bite was the favorite event of all the dogs, but I'd
learned on deployment that humans want to play
sook constantly, and Trainer Ben was no exception.
Almost every afternoon the dads loaded us into the
compartments in the back of a truck to go play.

We drove southeast, passing hills of sand on a warm
day in April. When the dads found a patch of dirt they
liked, the car stopped and we leapt out. We barely had
time to sniff the area before the dads challenged us to
race up to the top of a brushy mountain.

"Run them hard, get them winded,"Trainer Ben yelled
from behind us. "In combat they will be panting when
they are searching for explosives – we need to train
how we fight."

Everyone reached the peak, wheezing for air, and
before I could catch my breath, Dad had me sooking,
hiking over rubble and through thorny bushes to find
bombs.

I was used to these games, played with several "*sook*"
reminders and only a few rewards. I leaned into every
patch of shade, eventually finding a goal odor that
won me a tennis ball and a bowl of water. Just down
the path I found my second score. Dad poured water
on my pads and back, and I shook it right back at him
before we *sooked* for the game's third and final tennis
ball.

We returned to the car and rested; Hammer arrived next, desperate for a drink; his dad was complaining about the amount of time they'd spent checking out trash. Speedy and Jazz ran up next, followed a little while later by a tired and mellow Loki. Puppy Ace bounded up to us without any wins because he had forgotten the rules of the game – again. Storm straggled up last, out of shape since deployment – his heavy panting had distracted his nose, and he'd only found two of the three hidden odors. But each time we played the crew finished with better scores than the last.

****

The new training regime was realistic, and hard on my joints; I reinjured my wrist pretty much every day, but I wanted to be with Dad. Our practices were still easier than deployment, and we spent our nights tossing a ball on the beach. Some of my kennelmates had it tougher – a quick meal after practice followed by a night in lock up.

One evening at practice, Dad and I searched for the elusive Trainer Ben in a dark patch of desert thick with dry brush and shriveled trees. Dad sent me on a *"find em"* mission, and at the top of a crest I caught a whiff of sweat – then a flash of padding diving behind a boulder. I ran through the chaparral, sprinting towards Trainer Ben's potato body odor.

Just as I vaulted onto the boulder he was hiding behind, I felt a jagged branch stab me in the chest. I continued forward, undeterred, snapping off the piece that was wedged in my armpit as I leapt to ambush Trainer Ben from above. We were struggling when I felt his body tense.

"Hey! HEY! Where the hell is all this blood coming from?" Trainer Ben yelled.

Dad hurdled up the rocks behind me, calling for me to *"los!"* I released and he took me to a clearing where he pulled the wood spike out from the folds of my skin. After cleaning it out with water, he packed it with cloth and carried me to the car. I lay down to lick the pain, which hurt only slightly more than my always-angry wrist.

We drove home, past my favorite park— I whined but Dad would not stop. When we got inside, he assembled his medical gear on the kitchen floor and told me to lie down on a towel – then he squirted liquid into the wound and pulled the rest of the barbs out. I wiggled and tried to get up, assuring him that I could lick it clean, but Mom coaxed me back down on the floor. Dad worked on the area with great focus; I yelped when he pricked me but then the pain was gone, and Dad stitched the skin to stay shut.

The soreness dulled to a twinge. I rose for dinner and

a walk around the neighborhood before I curled up for a quiet night on the couch. The next morning I felt good as new and suggested we play a game of tug, but Dad made me rest and sit out a few days of training.

When I returned to the kennel house, Speedy was still in the neighboring cage. Our dads were friends, so we spent a lot of time together. Once I healed, our dads would take us on morning jogs down the beach, where we raced after tennis balls and through ocean waves, alerting each other to finds that one of us usually ate. Speedy was the rare dog that could keep up with me, both of us blessed with the quickness that inspired our names. Passing dogs sometimes accused us of ambush, but we ignored them – it was summer at the beach, and we were running, free, out of the kennel.

Speedy could relax on those days; but in the kennel house he became frustrated, on edge. Speedy was smart and well trained, but he was also still wild, easily offended, and raised to be tough. Upon joining our program, Speedy's luck had changed; his dad Mick treated him like family, sharing food and opening his home to him. Speedy loved his dad – he'd do anything for him – and that's why they were one of our top scoring teams.

Once Speedy had experienced life with Mick, he couldn't go back to lockup; but then one day Mick disappeared on a trip, leaving him in the kennel house full time. Speedy was devastated. For two weeks he dug holes in the yard, trying to escape and track down his dad. He never got anywhere; he just ended up having to sleep on lumpy ground with dirt wedged under his claws.

When the crew arrived to give us morning meals and recess, Speedy ran around checking the fence boundaries. When it came time to return to his kennel Speedy refused, demanding he be released to find Mick. This strategy always backfired – the dads forced him to return to his cage, and he got less free time at the next recess. When Mick finally returned Speedy was overjoyed, but damage had been done.

At practice, Speedy struggled with nerves, and it made him impulsive. One evening, the dogs were taking turns sniffing out bombs in small structures alongside a pack of dads, just like we did in Afghanistan. Mick brought Speedy out for his turn and gave him a *"sook,"* sending him racing through the dim passages in search of an odor.

As the event played out, I watched Dad walking around an exterior wall where he suddenly crossed paths with Speedy, who was turning a corner. Speedy looked up and was surprised to see a shadowy figure overhead – his jaws snapped frantically. Dad sprung backwards and commanded him to *"fooey!"* and *"sook!"* Later that same run, Speedy lashed out at another packmate's swinging arm, earning another angry *"fooey!"*

In the kennel that night I barked into Speedy's cage, telling him to stay away from my Dad – but he was too busy digging to respond. I finally gave up and fell asleep to the rhythm of Speedy's teeth grinding against the metal links of his cage.

****

Like most of the dogs in our kennel, I had grown up around other animals. In Holland, I lived with countless chickens, rabbits, and birds, and of course, the lawn-mowing goat. Ever since I almost decapitated myself chasing bunnies in Afghanistan and been sprayed in the face with toxic piss, I had gained a little perspective – unless I was provoked or really, really bored, I would be content to live and let live.

One morning, we took a long drive to the eastern mountain ranges, riding in small air-conditioned cabins along the side of a truck. The engine roar did not drown out the chorus of barks. Hammer bitched every time we banged our heads going over a pothole; Puppy Ace chirped about wanting to "tear it up out there," while the rest of us rolled our eyes. Speedy grumbled about the noise and cramped quarters, while Jazz sang a happy tune with a single, repeating verse. Loki roared about being tired of playing these damn games, interrupting his own tirade to tell Ace to shut up. I let out a sigh when we passed a lush grassy field, perfect for a game of catch, and wished my space was a couple of degrees cooler.

We pulled up to grassland that smelled of horse, sheep, cows, goats, rabbits and other woodland creatures. The doors opened to an air of stress and excitement, and we were immediately clipped to leashes. Jazz and I searched for goat turds; Ace spun in circles at the sight of some fast moving chickens. Loki's hunting instincts went into overdrive – before his dad could stop him, he'd run to the end of his 30-foot leash and crawled up a fence, teetering over the links and threatening a lamb below. The sheep below him bleated and bahhed as they tripped over each other to get to the opposite end of their pen. Loki's dad peeled him off the fence, yanking him a few times when he continued to menace his prey.

We began *sooking* drills on leash, and our dads gave us sharp corrections when our focus strayed from the event. Half a day of *sooking* and bite work later, everything started to disappear into the background – even puppy Ace learned to ignore the goat groupies he attracted. We started travelling to different farms once a week for practices, and eventually we were all able to compete in *sook* games without regard to our audience.

Back at our home training field, the lesson on avoiding other animals was reinforced. Our dads arrived at the kennel house one afternoon, and escorted Storm out alone. "*Take me too,*" Ace begged for a few minutes until all the residents settled into a quiet pause, ears alert to any noise on the field. There were no sounds of battle, so I assumed it was standard *sook* training until we heard Storm yelp. He returned to the kennel upset and twitchy.

Loki was taken out next, and returned later as though he'd gone out for a stroll. I barked at my Dad when he came to the kennel house, but he just waved and smiled before guiding Ace out to the field. Moments later we heard a wild scream, and Ace returned to the kennel with terror in his eyes.

I was up next – Dad reappeared and led me out on a leash. A few steps down the gravel road he stopped and clipped a heavy black collar on my neck, the kind Loki used to wear daily. I had only used this kind of necklace once before, to play a game where I ran to Dad when it vibrated.

We walked to the training field where we had played a thousand games, and this time we strolled around it aimlessly – a strange pageant, performed in front of the other dads. We made several wide loops before I discovered a new wooden crate near the parking lot. I approached, catching whiffs of hay, then the sweet musk of snake.

I stepped up to the box to peek through the wire netting, still sniffing. A sharp rattle startled me and I jumped back a little, but then I took another step closer. There was a glimpse of movement and then my collar zapped my neck hard – the current flowed down my spine and into my brain.

I cried out and ran back to Dad to report the attack. We returned to the kennel, where the other dogs were trying to make sense of the game. Ace babbled about being propelled into the sky by a shot of electricity. Hammer was outraged, and vowed to kill that snake

if he ever smelled him again. Speedy dug; Jazz and
I pouted quietly, and Loki waved off the entire thing,
calling it "weak shit," before he took a nap.

A few days later, we played the game again. The dads
came in to escort Speedy out to the training field – we
listened intently through a long pause – then a shriek.
Speedy returned, full of rage, and immediately began
digging a hole in the ground.

Dad appeared to release me next – we walked through
the gate and down towards the field. When he knelt
down to fasten the heavy collar around my neck I knew
this was the snake game and I didn't want to play. He
snapped the collar closed, but before he could attach
the leash I turned and sprinted down the gravel road,
past the cars and back to the kennel house. I sat there,
begging Dad to open the door and let me go back to
my cage.

"Turbo, here. *Here!*" Dad yelled. But I stood – I didn't
even look back at him.

His boots crunched down the path toward me. I was
surprised as he attached my leash that he wasn't mad –
he was actually trying not to smile. "Come on, boy," he
said, and we walked back over to the training field.

As we did the time before, Dad and I wandered around
the training field while the other dads watched. I

smelled a few pee posts and sniffed some odors in a drainage ditch. Then I caught a waft of sweet, musky hay, and I knew that damned snake was in the crate again, just waiting to attack me. Dad began walking towards its lair, but I strained in the opposite direction. Still curious, Dad kept guiding me over to the crate, but I turned my head away from it. I would never look at that snake again.

After several laps, the dads grew bored with our parade, so Dad gave me a "good boy" pat and declared me the winner. I had escaped the snake's wrath.

"Sorry guys, he's not going anywhere near that snake pen," Dad said.

"Hey, we can't fault him for being a fast learner." Trainer Ben said. Dad returned me to the kennel house – a champion of the snake game.

****

Our crew travelled to *sook* practices most days, so whenever our dads bypassed the truck and walked us out to the training field, I knew Trainer Ben would be meeting us there in his puffy suit.

One morning he introduced us to "fend-its" – obstacles he used to block our attack. Dad gave me a "*stellan*," but before I reached Trainer Ben he'd grabbed a chair and held it out between us, keeping me at a distance to avoid my bite. No matter how fast I ran I couldn't get around it – I spun him around until we were both dizzy.

Back at the kennel house the dogs were stumped – none of us had successfully gotten around the chair. Hammer had tried gnawing on its legs. Speedy, like me, had run in circles to no avail. Loki barked at the chair and Trainer Ben; he got in one quick nibble that didn't hold. Jazz nipped at Trainer Ben's feet as the chair continuously bonked him on the head.

But we kept playing, watching Trainer Ben's props, and eventually the openings began to appear. The first time I caught him, he was turning in one direction and I juked the other way to bite the back of his leg. He cursed and grabbed his hip as he submitted. In our next match, he pointed a trashcan at me and I darted underneath it. The can rolled across my back as I latched onto Trainer Ben's thigh. Dad went wild.

"Yaah, *braffy*! That's my boy!"

The other dogs also began finding their way around the fend-its, and everyone's timing and striking angles improved. Trainer Ben's calves were almost always exposed, and a lot of us had gotten good at getting under the fend-its without getting hit. A good way to handle large objects was usually a deceptive maneuver, running the human in one direction and then switching back for a bite. Ace was the only dog in our crew who continued to have trouble, but it wasn't from lack of effort – he ran in circles around Trainer Ben, bouncing and babbling, "*put down the trashcan and fight, chicken!*"

Trainer Ben continued to raise the intensity. A few months into training, he suited up and waddled down the field – then he turned and growled at me. Dad gave me a pep talk and a chest thump before unclipping my leash with a "*stellan!*" I sprinted down the course, my eyes watching the center of the suit for movement. Trainer Ben's leg rose into a block-kick defense, and I switched my aim to the exposed inner thigh, hitting the groin and extracting a grunt. We thrashed around; he did some spins and landed a couple of glancing smacks.

Suddenly Trainer Ben grabbed my inner thigh, pinching a fold of skin in his fist. I bit down harder at first, but the pain in my leg became so intense that I let go with a yelp. Trainer Ben's hands wrenched down harder, and I thought of my fight in Afghanistan – *the fear of failure.* Then I stared down at Trainer Ben's hand, and with a surge of rage I hit his arm. My jaws clamped down with such raw power I thought I might rip it off his body. Trainer Ben immediately released his grip on my leg, squirming in surrender.

"*Los!* That's a good boy – that's my *br-r-raffy!*"

Dad declared me the winner, and the other dads congratulated me with head pats.

Trainer Ben started putting all of the tricks we'd learned together during my bite events – he would use a trashcan fend me off, and I would dart underneath it or fake left and bite right. If he grabbed a hunk of my skin, I went after the arm doing the gripping. If he flung me off of him, I spun around and attacked a spot he couldn't defend. His angry growls were part of the fun.

As the fights became more advanced, our dads started to jump in, helping us beat up Trainer Ben. I loved it when Dad tapped into my fight – he had my back – but other dogs weren't so trusting. After years of being choked, Loki didn't welcome his dad creeping up on him mid-fight, and he kept one eye on him. And the first time Hammer's dad joined the fight Hammer looked at him and grumbled, "*you're next.*"

Even Speedy became nervous when Mick first intervened to kick and punch Trainer Ben – he hopped away from him, his mouth still on the bite, just in case Mick turned on him too. But soon it was common – a welcome gesture – and the dads became superheroes when they swooped in; it made our crew of dogs and dads more of a pack. Speedy beamed with pride when his dad joined him; and Jazz and his dad beat up Trainer Ben together like a couple of giddy schoolyard bullies.

Storm and his dad were a good team, with a shared love of pizza; but fighting was never Storm's best event. His initial takeoff and bite landings were good, and his dad jumping in gave him a boost – but as Trainer Ben's courses grew more intense, Storm lost interest. He hated the entrapment maneuver – where Trainer Ben would flip us over and pin us on our backs, laying on top of us like a heavy blanket. The rest of us would try to wiggle out from under him, but Storm would just forfeit – lying still and waiting for it to be over. When Trainer Ben grabbed his skin or threatened any pain, Storm quit.

Storm's performance on the *sook* field began to suffer as well. He started out sniffing the landscape with shallow breaths – not the deep inhales of a search. Soon after he would hone in on a spot – usually a food smell, an old soda can – and plop down with an expression that said, "*Are we done?*" Trainer Ben would shake his head, but Storm would try to convince his dad that the location was a game winner, his eyes fixed on the "spot." Eventually he would admit there was nothing there.

Storm was tired. The practices were physically demanding – he wasn't the athlete he once was. Aches and pains plagued his body. He'd returned from deployment to sleepless nights; and when he did sleep, something was chasing him through his dreams. He wanted peace, quiet, and a spot on his dad's couch where he could grow a belly. A month later, his wishes were granted – Storm retired from the program, and was adopted by his dad.

****

When Dad's facial fur grew shaggy, I knew we were preparing for another deployment. We competed in a large San Diego tournament with the other dads – everyone dressed in full game gear – where we racked up many victories. Then our practices stopped, and the pile making began. Our gear was thick and heavy this go-round, full of goose-feather vests and boots made of cowhide. Mom also made piles – stacks of food, sealed in airtight bags.

As October came to a close, Mom announced that we would be celebrating the holidays early this year; and she and Dad covered the house in lights. They moved a tree into the living room and trimmed it with glitter. Mom made a feast of buttery treats; we ate turkey and napped on our backs with our stuffed bellies in the air.

Later that night, we opened boxes that had collected under the tree. I pulled treats, toys, and a black puffy vest out of my gift-wrappings, and all of it was added to the piles.

I fell asleep on the couch and woke the next morning to a cloudy November dawn. Dad loaded up the car and "*hooged*" me into the back where I leapt into a kennel wedged between the bags of game gear.

We drove down to the airfield to listen for the C-130. Dad was lost in thoughts about the games; Mom's eyes were sad. She pestered me with hugs and kisses – the kind usually reserved for bedtime – and told me to take care of my Dad. I waved her off to explore the area, and she went to nuzzle Dad, making him promise we would return home safe.

A short time later, Speedy and Mick joined us on the dusty tarmac. Speedy and I sprinted a few laps along the sand berms, peeing on every post, before our dads led us into our kennels for the long plane ride. I watched Mom's car disappear in the distance; then we were loaded onto the plane and ascended into the clouds, headed to round two of the deployment games.

Chapter 7
Afghanistan Redux

Our trip started with a layover in Virginia. Dad
checked us into a hotel where we each had our own
bed; Speedy and Mick shared the room next door.
After breakfast, Dad and I walked to a stretch of beach
nearby where we could throw the ball around. In the
afternoon we met up with our new pack for a practice
run; and at night, Dad visited one of his old packmates.
They howled late into the night, with whiskey heavy on
their breath.

A couple of nights later, Dad and Mick went out for
a meal, leaving Speedy and me alone in our rooms. I
napped, listening for the sound of Dad's return, but all
I could hear was the racket next door. A series of pings,
and then grunts, then pings again… I dozed in and out
of consciousness.

Suddenly, thunderous stomping – Speedy running laps
around his room. After a number of passes over the
bedsprings, the room quieted again. Then a thump
next door turned into a steady rhythm of knocking,
timed to Speedy's jumps. I was mildly curious about
his antics, but mainly I wanted him to be quiet so I

could hear when Dad returned.

I awoke again to a loud whack and a thud, followed by a lazy creak. My eyes opened – the door to our room was still closed. With a disappointed sigh, I shut my eyes and listened to galloping in the hall – steps that grew softer as he ran to one end, and then escalated again as they passed my room.

I hopped off the bed and stretched my stiff legs before walking over to sniff the gap under the door; I confirmed Speedy was doing sprints in the hallway and then returned to my warm spot on the bed.

Dad returned a short time later. "Hello, *braffy!*"

I scrambled off the bed and ran over to him to stick my nose in his face, sniffing his dinner, but there was a clatter at our door. It swung back open and Mick careened into our room, yelling, "Speedy's missing! He broke out of his cage."

It wasn't news to me, but we ran next door to see the mauled kennel, its metal door hanging loosely from one hinge. Dad pointed to a blinking light on the phone, and Mick picked it up – his expression shifting from panic to confusion.

"It was a message from the front desk," he said. "They have Speedy up there."

The three of us took the elevator down to the lobby, where we saw Speedy's tail waving us over, inviting us to meet his new friends. A woman with long brown hair pinned back into a tail on her head was smiling at us.

"He's fine," she said as we approached. "He just appeared, so we kept him back here with us until you returned. I gave him some treats – I hope you don't mind."

After a round of apologies, Mick escorted Speedy back to the elevator. "How the hell did he get out of the room?" Dad asked.

"How did he get from the fourth floor down to the front desk?" Mick asked in an even higher pitch.

I knew that Speedy had tracked Mick's smell to the elevator, and some humans let him on because he knew where he was going. He probably would have greeted Dad and Mick at the restaurant, but the lady at the front desk distracted him with food. We just found him at a pit stop.

****

Dad and I woke early the next morning, and he
wrestled our bags to a waiting van where we met
up with Speedy and Mick. The sun peaked out for a
moment, but not long enough to warm the November
air, so Dad zipped me into my new fleece vest. We
boarded the first of several flights and arrived on a
familiar, rocky airstrip – icy gusts of jet fuel and shit
swamps filled my nostrils.

It was winter in Afghanistan, and the frozen ground
was no better a host to grass than the parched dirt had
been in the summer. We spent a couple of nights at
our old campground searching out familiar pee posts
and packmates before we said goodbye to Speedy and
Mick.

A truck took us out to the airfield, where Dad and I caught a flight to the middle of the desert, landing at a small encampment – our new pack was there, buzzing around, moving tents and building piles. Several local players had also joined our team, milling around camp and shooting me uneasy looks.

We only spent a couple of nights living there in a crowded tent before the whole camp collapsed and was loaded into a caravan of vehicles and trucks that stretched so far down the road I couldn't see its end. Dad and I were given the back two seats of a "MATV" – a beige truck that was shaped like Loki's fat head. Dad strapped me into a seat behind a couple of packmates, and then he focused on the control panel for the big gun above us. The warm air inside the vehicle was a swirling mixture of gunpowder, sweat and chocolate.

I spent the morning watching the MATVs, trucks and a stretch of trailers ahead crawling over hills and jostling through potholes. The line moved slowly – a herd of elephants lumbering through a rugged piece of desert. The heater kept my paws warm as the car bounced down the hard-packed road.

The sun reached the top of the sky when we saw a massive fireball up ahead – followed by a deep boom – blasting its way through one of the mammoth trucks. The rig tumbled off the side of the road in slow motion, smoke gushing out into the empty sky.

Dad grabbed a medical bag and we leapt out of the car, running towards the heap of metal slumped over in a ditch by the road. Some pack members ran up with us; others stayed behind, scanning the hills for opponents. I knew from the odor that one of the local players had been driving – he was in pieces now, and nothing in Dad's bag could fix that. Pack members surveyed the crater under the car while Dad and I *sooked* the area for more traps.

We returned to our MATV and watched a forklift push the mangled truck upright. A tow moved into place, and the convoy started to creep forward like a caterpillar – stretching out over terrain as we built momentum – then scrunching to a stop when the pack spotted a disturbed pad of dirt up ahead. Dad and I were called to the front to sniff the road for bombs before the convoy could proceed. The breeze chilled my nose as I *sooked*, and rocks wedged between my numb pads – I found them later, after I raced Dad back to the car.

I found three more explosive dumps in the road, and the pack blew them all up. Our radios predicted more traps ahead, and after a long huddle the pack abandoned the route. Our vehicles shuffled, turned around, and finally began moving forward again as the sun touched down on the horizon.

We returned the same way we came, so Dad and I

stayed warm all the way back to the campground we'd left that morning, arriving long after dark. Dad built a tent, only to take it down a short nap later when the pack rose to resume our journey at dawn.

This time we moved southeast, where our machines struggled through the pillowy sand dunes, their wheels sinking into the powder. Our caravan ground to a halt several times as we watched packmates tie thick ropes to bumpers, tugging the giants forward so the line could proceed. By the time evening fell, we seemed to have made less progress than we would have on foot. The cavalry of trucks parked in a circle and we set up camp in the middle.

With no fire for warmth or light, Dad and I snuggled into a tent, surrounded by silent, foreign land. I tried desperately to sleep and ignore my own shivering – the blankets and pads provided little buffer from the frozen desert floor.

A couple of hours later, Dad and I were tagged for "watch." We emerged from the balmy tent – it was cold outside, but the wind had stopped – and shuffled over to the MATV, where we traded spots with a packmate. Inside the warm cabin, I burrowed into a seat while Dad stared at the screens next to me. The cold melted away and I slept, waking when the door opened and I was hit with a blast of cold air – and we were evicted to return to our frosty tent.

The caravan rolled out at first light, chugging along until the wheels of a truck up ahead started spinning in the dirt. We stopped to watch other vehicles tug it out, and as soon as one was free, another would get stuck. The hours passed by almost as slowly as we advanced. Dad and I took turns walking security, and sometimes we *sooked* the path forward, but the only thing ahead of us that day was infinite sand. We stopped to set up another temporary camp in the desert; the highlight of my night was a warm nap in the vehicle while Dad stood watch.

On the third, windy day of our trek, a pallet fell out of a plane overhead and landed on the desert floor. The convoy halted and the pack formed a line extending to the drop spot, passing boxes of food and game equipment into the rear of a truck. Dad and I busied ourselves *sooking* the area, Dad's face reddening from the sandblasts.

We returned to the vehicle and drove for a few hours until a fireball tore through the truck we'd just loaded, blowing our new supplies into the sky. Dad and I jumped out of our MATV and ran towards the smoke plume as the rest of the pack took up security positions. Burned plastic and food particles rained down around us.

The driver, a local player, was alive – but his leg was missing and his arm was dangling by a thin flap of skin. The pack moved his body into a clearing where Dad kneeled down to examine his wounds. I watched from behind Dad's shoulder as he pulled bandages and medicines from his bag; then I wandered over to sniff the leg that had been thrown a good distance from the patient's body – it smelled of smoke and singed hair; the muscles inside were beginning to die. Dad stuck the man with a needle and then twisted a bandage down hard onto his leg – the injured player let out a sleepy whimper as the gush of blood slowed to a trickle.

Dad turned and unclipped my leash. "Turbo, *sook!*"

I darted around the area searching for bombs, running all the way to the front of the convoy where I found a draft that I followed right back to the crater under the truck; I sat.

Dad looked over his shoulder at me and responded, "Yes, I know this area smells like explosives. Good boy. *Sook!*"

I dashed back out into the desert, but the odors kept leading me back to Dad. There were no other finds in the area.

"That's a good boy," he said, his eyes still focused on the wounded man. I sat and watched Dad work to reattach the limp arm back onto his shoulder.

One of the other local players approached us, his face concerned – he motioned to me a number of times as he spoke. The terp translated his words.

"He asks, should the dog be that close? What if he bites him?"

Dad kept his eyes on a hole he was packing with gauze. "Tell him not to worry. Turbo won't hurt him."

Then Dad turned back to look at me. "Turbo, *sit. Bliven.*"

I planted my butt on the cold ground. Dad reattached my leash and continued bandaging the man's swelling skin. The blood clotted quickly in the cold air, and the man drifted to sleep as Dad and others lifted him onto a stretcher, holding up a bag of fluid that was attached to his arm. When the helicopter arrived, the pack loaded him onboard before it zipped off into the sky.

We spent the remainder of that day pulling vehicles out of the dirt and making short advances. I found one hidden trap in the road that the pack blew up – we toured the smoldering spot as our vehicles crawled by, building up to walking speed. Finally, exhausted and weathered, we stopped in the desert for another freezing night in our tent, looking forward to our turn in the watch car.

****

We drove on, slogging through soft earth and avoiding further casualties. On the sixth day, one of our forklifts blew up – Dad and I hurried to the pile of rubble and were happy to discover our packmate, though deaf, was still in one piece.

After spending seven long days covering only ten miles of ground, we arrived at the barren piece of desert that was our final destination. Guys exited the cars, complaining of aching backs from hours stuck in cramped seats; their faces were calloused and red from the elements. We circled the caravan and crawled back into our tents for another frigid, sleepless night.

We woke at dawn to begin building our camp. The pack pushed dirt with machines and erected wire walls filled with sandbags. Huge tents were raised, attached to engines that pumped them full of warm air. Dad tied my leash to a post, and from there I watched my packmates haul piles all over camp. By the time the stars were peaking out of the dimming sky, our pack had outfitted the empty land with several beige canvas buildings and barricades. Retiring to a heated tent, Dad and I settled in for our first real night of sleep in a week.

Days of busy camp building followed – tents multiplied, and were filled up with computers, screens, game gear, and food. The pack started work when the morning light was faint, before it got rosy; they continued until the cold night air made their hands stiff. We retired to the tents coated in dust, and collapsed into our bunks, but our sleep was interrupted every night by watches – Dad wrapping us in puffy vests to walk the perimeter of the new camp, his goggles and gun scanning the hills. I tried relentlessly to steer us back toward the tent, but I never won that battle.

A week after we arrived at our new campsite, the tournament commenced. Dad suited up in armor and zipped my competition vest over my fleece; we met up with the pack just before dawn. We split into two teams – the other crew trekked up the steep mountains to the west, while the rest of us walked down a timeworn road to "Sadeek Village." Dad unleashed me to run ahead *sooking* for bombs, but the dirt was only scented with fuel and livestock.

As the sun rose over the hills, we came to a cluster of adobe compounds, where we played a familiar game – our terp announced the rules and told everyone to exit the village if they did not want to participate. Women and children flooded out followed by a number of men; they looked at us suspiciously as we herded them to the side yard. Our local players – the pack called them "ANAs"– competed in the first round of the event, exiting the compound without any points. Then Dad sent me in with a *sook* command and the pack followed. I *sooked* all of the rooms, investigating woven rugs, rusty stoves, china cabinets, and even a goat wandering through the courtyard – I found no bombs and no opponents.

That was when the game changed – the pack settled in to talk to the villagers while I searched the yard for rabbit turds and pee hubs. Talk was tense, polite, questioning... when we left, the Sadeek villagers still seemed a little unsure about us, but friendly tones were exchanged.

We returned on the same road we'd traveled to Sadeek, but on the trip back I pulled Dad towards the smell of explosives. The wind was coming from behind me, so I doubled back to sniff a drainage ditch next to the road. Just as my butt was lowering to the ground, Dad called me to him and a tennis ball popped out of his hand. I chewed it while the pack checked out the spot and surrounding footprints, nodding and pointing.

They stacked white bricks on top of the odor. Dad covered my ears, and it exploded once – then a second time with even greater force. A plume of black and yellow smoke gathered under the gray clouds above.

"That's a good boy," he said, thumping me on the chest before releasing me to *sook* the rest of the way to camp.

The next afternoon we headed out on foot again,

sooking the road several miles beyond Sadeek. It was
December now, and the chalky wind chafed our faces
as we patrolled down the road on numb feet. I was
happy to walk, even with my achy knees and hips, and
avoid the dizzy, screaming helicopters; but with huge
bags strapped to their backs, the pack probably would
have preferred to get a ride.

A cluster of structures came into view, and some of our
packmates broke off to climb the surrounding hills.
Dad told me to *sook* as we crossed over a stream and
into a green valley with many trees; I found no hidden
bombs. When our terp requested the villagers leave
the compound, most did so calmly; only a few men,
including one elder with a large, fuzzy beard, were
irritated by our visit. Our search of the village resulted
in no finds, but we checked out some of their papers.

The pack called the compound "clear", and the elder
invited them to sit; they gathered to kneel on a rug
placed in the compound's entrance. The elder spoke
in stern commands through his thick purple beard –
explanations and demands were exchanged – but after
much effort by the terp, the elder's heavily charcoaled
eyes remained skeptical.

Bored with all the chatter, I sniffed the food table until
Dad gave me a *"fooey."* When the bearded elder invited
us to stay and eat I would have happily accepted his
offer – but the pack wasn't as hungry; they only ate a

few bites. Dad handed me a grilled hunk of goat and I swallowed it whole before we started the long hike back to camp, leaving the delicious feast behind.

****

Every couple of days we visited another village. At the new ones, we made our standard announcements and searched for bombs; at those we'd already checked, we just stopped to visit with the villagers. Some of them were wary of us, but no one seemed eager to fight – we rarely heard the pops and booms that were common during our last deployment tournament. Either the game had changed, or everyone was just too cold to play.

One brutally cold morning in late December we woke early – Dad helped to raise the walls of another new camp building while I cruised around looking for food before returning to the tent and my warm bed. Dad woke me a couple of hours later, and we geared up for an afternoon walk to Sadeek.

The wind whipped across the well-traveled road – the air was so cold my eyeballs felt glassy, almost frozen. We hiked the familiar walk and greeted the villagers – most of them had no interest in me besides staying out of my leash range. After some discussion with the pack, the village elder called the children together, and one of our packmates fished through his bag, handing out colored pencils, shirts, and soccer balls.

The children held up their rewards and shared them with the other villagers. People relaxed; some of the moms smiled. I tried to snag a soccer ball, but Dad gave me my tennis ball instead.

The pack left Sadeek that day in high spirits. We returned to camp – our heated tent – and Dad ate his dinner out of a plastic bag. We snacked on some goodies that Mom sent us, and then we went outside to set the camp's poop collection on fire before bedtime.

After the "Christmas" op, Sadeek villagers began visiting our camp, too. One afternoon, the pack alerted Dad to a man who had arrived with a bullet in his stomach. Dad grabbed his medical bag and we ran to another tent where we found the man lying down, covered in blood. Dad examined the wounds as he talked to our terp.

The injured man stared up at me as Dad packed him full of cotton and stuck a needle in his arm, handing the attached bag to a packmate who held it up high in the air. Dad stuck a rubber straw up his nose and the breathing became peaceful; then he propped up the man's legs and covered him with a blanket. A little while later, a helicopter arrived – the pack loaded him up, and he floated away.

Another day, members of a more remote village appeared on the road to our camp, their arms loaded with food. I welcomed a home-cooked meal, but the pack was wary; they only allowed them to enter after we'd patted their robes down. After a talk with our terp the feast was taken to camp's galley, and the pack thanked the villagers as they headed back down the road to their home.

I passed over the cucumbers to get a whiff of the meat dishes, pleading with Dad for a bite; but he refused to share, probably still annoyed about my earlier attempt to get a taste of the camp's poo pit. Suddenly one of our packmates yelped – he spit out a hunk of chicken, and then felt around inside his mouth – pulling out a metal needle.

The pack was abuzz, angry. They voted to send the food to the dump. I wanted to take my chances, but Dad ignored me as he checked out our packmate's bleeding gums. They examined the needle and discussed it with voices on the radio; not long after, a helicopter came to whisk him away. He returned a few days later in good health – but Dad still refused to let me get the chicken out of the trash.

****

It wasn't until late January that we found some opponents who wanted to play – and our pack was happy to accept the challenge.

Dad and I suited up to meet our team over by the new

vehicles, and when the radios told us where we would be playing, we drove towards the rising sun. I sat on the floorboards of a buggy, wedged between Dad's legs, hitting my head on the dashboard at every bump. Cold air whipped through the car's open frame. Dad wrapped his coat around me, but it was a miserable ride for both of us.

Our caravan slowed to a halt several times while everyone waited for Dad and I to *sook* suspicious stretches of road. I was happy to *sook* – it was warmer than the car ride. I scored one ball for a find buried near a drainage ditch, and I chewed it while our packmates arranged their pile of explosive bricks. Dad coaxed me back into our vehicle, which jolted away from the scene as a fireball shot high into the sky behind us.

We resumed our wild ride, arriving at a village nestled between orchards, surrounded by the smell of rich soil. We approached the first compound where our terp's announcements triggered an exodus of women and children – they were not happy about our visit, and even less happy about my presence. Dad sent me in for a *"find em,"* and I raced through the building with the pack. There were no players inside, so Dad sent me back through for a bomb *sook*.

I was examining the kitchen when we heard pops and rumbles nearby, and our radios crackled to life. Dad and I hurried to the vehicles, and drove north past crops and structures to another village. The cars rolled to a stop in front of an eroding wall, and I heard a buzz of people inside.

A couple of our mates stayed back at the roof guns on the cars while the rest of us snuck into the compound's maze, on the lookout for opponents. As we passed through, moms grabbed their kids and steered them into rooms to get them away from the game. We ran to a large building in the middle of the village, and packmates spread out, guarding the corner flanks.

"*Find em!*" Dad said, as he swung the heavy wooden door open. I ran in, through a lobby and down a hallway where I found several small rooms lined with floormats, but no opponents. When he told me to *sook* I ran straight to the third room down the hall and sat next to a metal box. The pack found a large gun stash, which we confiscated before running back out to the courtyard.

The pack immediately keyed up on a group of men who were peeking at us from behind a nearby building – as the pack whispered into their radios, the suspects darted out into the open, spraying us with their guns. We ducked behind a wall as dust puffed into the air around us; then the gun rhythm stopped and the pack charged out, showering our opponents with bullets as they scampered off.

Our radios directed us not to follow them, so we moved to another building, where Dad sent me in with a *"sook."* I sniffed for bombs among the furniture, pottery and floormats and didn't find any traps – but I did smell opponents behind a colorful, hanging rug.

I sniffed all around it, nudging it to one side, but I couldn't find anyone. I smelled odor seeping from a crack in the wall, so I barked an alert to Dad. He came in, gun drawn and confused.

"Hey, Turbo's found something, get in here," he yelled.

The pack filtered in, with guns at their noses. Dad pulled the rug back to uncover a panel in with the wall. Tension was high as Dad prepared to kick it – the pack was ready to attack.

The door clattered open, and we heard muffled whimpers. Tucked inside was a huddle of three children, a mom, and a couple of men. Guns still raised, the pack ushered them out of the cubby – their faces were upset, their eyes averted as they passed. They shuffled off with the terp, speaking in hushed tones. I knew they lived here – the floormats in the back room smelled just like them.

The radios called, so we said goodbye to the family and hustled out of the village, tracking our opponents down to the riverbed. I could smell their stench on a breeze, and my legs vibrated in anticipation.

Dad turned to the terp and whispered, "Tell them that they can surrender now, or we will send the dog in after them."

The terp shouted a message that echoed off the mountains in the distance; we listened to silence, then a few bird songs. As the seconds passed, I could feel Dad preparing to unclip my leash – and I shot forward as soon as the words *"find em!"* escaped his mouth.

My feet pounded as I sailed through the trees. I detected a smell to my left, the crunch of rocks ahead, a flash across my field of vision – and my legs made adjustments. I followed my opponents around a bend of trees, my feet slapping the water, numb to the underlying bed of stones. I closed in until my opponents' shadows were just a few feet ahead.

I charged up behind their team's slowest runner and sped into a launch – when I struck, the force of my hit knocked him forward. We slid to a stop in the dirt, with my jaws attached just under his left buttocks. His thigh was hard and sinewy without a puffy suit, and his warm blood leaked out on my scrunched tongue.

He screamed while his foot searched frantically for my body. He landed two kicks to my ribs – I released my first bite, spun around, and bit his calf, just under

195

his knee – he cried out. My top teeth dug in, tearing through tendons and ligaments. He flipped over, scraping me against the river rocks as he tried to balance his body upright and steady the gun in his hand. I released his knee and surged towards his face, attacking his forearm.

As we wrestled, I heard branches rustling – the other opponents were calling out, their voices close. Then I heard the pack patrol up behind me – a series of snaps cracked over my head – and my opponent stopped fighting. His arm dropped to the ground as the body fell limp.

"*Los!*" Dad said, and I stepped back, sniffing the blood that was pooling at my feet. The pack frisked the cooling body and took his weapon. Our terp called out to the other opponents still hidden in the trees, asking whether they wanted to keep playing – we heard their weapons hit the dirt with a thud before they emerged into a clearing.

The losing team was instructed to remove their clothes and fall to their knees; they raised empty hands in the air and the pack's guns surrounded their heads. Dad told me to "*watch em*" as their hands were cuffed behind their backs. Adrenaline dulled a nagging pain in my leg, my focus entirely on our rivals as the pack walked them up the hill and back to our vehicles. I was ready to pounce on any sudden movements, but our opponents were no longer in the mood to play.

****

Despite the freezing temperatures, Dad and I walked the camp perimeter every night, kicking dust that hung in the air, suspended under the clouds of our breath. I odor mapped the camp and left my markings; Dad talked to Mom on the telephone, and we sometimes we stopped to chat with a teammate. We saw fewer people out when the rains came, and the dirt turned into clay – it dried into hard wedges between my toes and crumbled off into my bed.

Dad and I also patrolled the camp on watch every other night – he would climb up into a tower and scan the area while I shivered below, whining about my raw pads. My vest was warm, but sharp breezes passed through it like spilt ice water.

As the weeks passed, the rain turned into snowflakes and I started to dread our watch turns. Sound asleep, I would feel a draft of cold air sweep across the floor – the tent door was open – and then I'd hear someone creeping over to Dad's cot. A hoarse whisper, and then Dad would rise slowly, his joints popping from the blood flow.

He would put on his puffy jacket and game gear, then turn to me to ask, "Are you ready, buddy?"

Most of the time I got up, stretched and rallied; some nights, I lifted my head to ask for five more minutes. Dad would smile and say, "Okay. I'll see you in an hour."

Dad and I lived in a tent with three packmates, all of whom were friendly with scratches, pets, and snacks. Each had a cot and a sleeping bag, shelves with food, and hooks for gear. They played music and had many visitors – packmates who sat on our maze of metal boxes. There was a lot of laughing.

Our roommates were also tagged for watches during the night. I would hear footsteps crossing the room and stopping at a neighbor's bed. I listened to the shuffling, and when the tent door closed I would run over to snag the warm spot left behind. My neighbor returned to find me burrowed in his blankets, fast asleep. They would usually rattle the cot and send me back to my pad – unless it was Buck, my favorite roommate.

Buck would come back from watch and shake me a little, but then he'd take off his game gear and find an open spot. We slept like puppies.

The next morning, Dad found me there – I had the pillow, while Buck's feet dangled off the end of the bed, his head wedged into a warm space next to my butt.

"Next time, just push him off!" Dad told Buck as I got up and jumped off the bed.

Buck just shrugged. "He looked so comfortable, I didn't want to wake him." That's why he was my favorite.

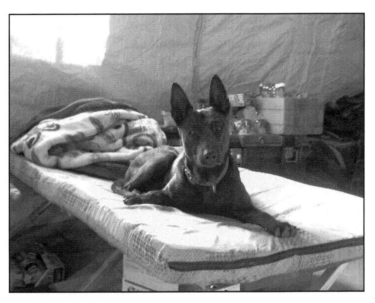

During our daily walks, I was always on the hunt for abandoned food around camp. The pack's food came in shiny brown plastic kits that dropped out of the sky on bulky palettes; wrappers and scraps were left on tables and scattered by the wind, and I was happy to help with the clean up. One of my favorite camp spots was the galley trashcan, full of intriguing smells – but sneaking food out of it was tough, because Dad became my opponent.

Some of the best smells in camp came from a green tent where the local players lived. Their dinners were not sealed in plastic, so smells of roasted goat and toasted bread billowed out of their chimney. But the locals kept their distance from me; they never offered friendly pets or food.

One night, Dad and I were touring the camp on a nighttime pee break, and he took my leash off so we could throw the ball down a long dirt pad. After a couple of throws, my tongue was coated in a sticky paste. On the third toss, I jumped to catch the ball, noting a whiff of smoke and meat on an easterly wind. Assessing the distance, I circled wide on my return lap, breaking right to duck behind a tent out of Dad's view – then I dropped the ball and sprinted towards the scent.

My nose directed me to the green tent with the great smoke plume hovering overtop. I heard the hum of people as I ran through the flap, but was greeted by a hush and shocked stares. I began searching the room as they sprung up from their floor mats and ran to the back wall of the tent, leaving plates of food behind. I scooped up as much of the feast as I could – huge gulps of goat, rice and vegetables. Dad was calling my name in the distance, so I didn't have time to chew.

I heard Dad's boots and the tent's flap slapping open. Dad's voice boomed through the door as I forced another bite of goat chunks down. "Turbo, *FOOEY!*"

I swallowed the last bite hard as Dad ran up and pulled me off the food, reconnecting my leash. He looked at the local players – some in green uniforms, others in long robes – whose eyes were all riveted on the twitch of my leg.

"I'm sorry." Dad repeated. His eyes scanned for our terp. "Please, tell them I'm sorry." The terp spoke, and some nodded; others were too scared to move.

But as the months passed, I started making some local friends. Our visits to Sadeek were frequent, and the children were curious – they began stalking me, watching my activities. One day a little boy talked to Dad through our terp, and based on their eyes, I knew the conversation was about me.

Dad was smiling. "Sure – I'll show them what he can do," he said.

He turned to me and we ran through our *"sit"* and *"aufliggen"* commands – the children were mildly pleased. Then Dad instructed me to *"gib-lout,"* opening and closing his fingers like a beak. I gave him a thunderous, throat-clearing bark.

The littlest kids took a few steps back, but the taller ones grinned with rows of craggy teeth. Dad gave me the command again, and I responded with a series of barks.

From that day on every time we visited Sadeek Village the kids swarmed around us, asking for a performance. Some adults even joined audience – at a distance – their faces worried at first, then interested, and finally amused. When one of the boys asked if he could pet my head, Dad told me to *"aufliggen."* I lay down as his little hand extended to touch my forehead, just barely, before it snapped back to his side. The other kids *"oohhhed,"* at his bravery. I didn't know what I had done, but Dad said I'd done it well and gave me a tennis ball.

During another visit, the pack was meeting with the village elders, our terp translating the exchange. I was attached to the long leash on Dad's hip, moving around the courtyard – I tracked the smell of hay and apples to a spread of goat turds scattered on the compound floor, and I sucked them up, snorting one up my nose.

Suddenly, the elder's words wavered and came to a halt – he spoke to the terp, who looked at Dad.

"He wants to know if you… feed your dog."

My ears perked at a familiar word, and my eyes met the stares from the pack. I saw confusion on Dad's face, then a smile as he said, "Yes, of course I feed him. Why?"

There was a back and forth between the elder and the terp before he responded, "He says, then why is he eating goat shit?"

All of the heads turned to me again as I nibbled my treats. I stood, chewing, trying to figure out why I had the group's attention. I waited for a command, but it never came.

The elder started laughing – a big, belly laugh. It was contagious – the other villagers caught it first, then it spread to the pack – sending a wave of lightness over the group. Moms and children giggled. I wasn't in on the joke, so I went back to harvesting my candies.

Later that week, our entire camp was shrouded by a dust storm. The wind whipped the sand into a dense

fog, and everything got lost in the haze. When Dad
and I took our morning walk, I did my business quickly,
blinking the crud out of my eyes. We hurried back to
our tent, eating breakfast and listening to music with
our roommates – then we heard people calling for the
medic.

Dad grabbed his bag and we ran outside to find two
Sadeek villagers; one of them had blood leaking out of
his chest. The wounded man moved slowly, struggling
to breathe in the thick air. The pack carried him to
a tent and laid him down on a floormat so that Dad
could examine his mouth, nose and eyes.

Dad took a needle out of his bag, angled, and stabbed
it into the man's chest. Hot gas hissed out; the injured
villager took a couple of big gulps of air, and color
flooded back into his face. His breathing calmed. Dad
cleaned his chest and plugged the wound with gauze,
his sleeves turning purple. I sat by his side, next to
another packmate who held up the medicine bag
draining into the man's arm.

Dad turned to the villager who had helped escort our
patient. "You need to get this man to a hospital. We
can't call in the helicopters in this storm – you need to
drive him there right now."

The villager nodded, thanking Dad – his hands pressed
together, his mouth and eyes smiling. The injured man

also nodded, weak from the medicine. Dad injected two vials into the bag and covered his wounds before closing the man's robes to keep him warm. We loaded him into the villager's truck, and it disappeared into a dirt cloud.

On our next visit to Sadeek, something had changed. We visited them on a cold, clear February day, and when we approached the compound, we were greeted as guests. The men gave us nods, and the moms and children smiled and bowed their heads. The elder emerged to express his gratitude to Dad for caring for their friend during the dust storm. He explained that the wounded man was the village teacher; that he had made it to the hospital and survived. The elder kept repeating a phrase, pointing at Dad with open hands.

"What is he saying?" Dad asked.

Our terp's eyes flashed up to the sky, searching for the words. "He says you are the Dog Angel," he explained. "That is what they call you. You are the one who saved the teacher – the Dog Angel."

From that day on, we heard that phrase, even in other villages –"Dog Angel." Even the moms – generally not my biggest fans – looked at me with soft eyes. They offered us gifts of food, and the kids begged us to perform our obedience games. Suddenly everyone wanted to play.

****

We continued to visit villages looking for pick-up games, but the nights of ear-piercing blasts seemed like a distant memory – our opponents' energy was focused on finding new and creative hiding places for their explosives. As a result, Dad and I spent long hours walking in front of convoys, charting odors in the road – and no matter the aches, I pressed on without whining. I didn't want Dad to start playing without me.

Early one grey morning, our cars sped down a bumpy road, stopping often to allow Dad and me to *sook* the path ahead. I leapt out to investigate an area while the

pack huddled on the side of the road, pointing up at
two caves dug into the top of the eastern hills. When
we returned to our vehicles, we drove off-road into
the scrub, bouncing over the vertical terrain. The cars
crunched to a stop at a small dirt pad.

A few packmates stayed back with the vehicles' roof
guns while Dad and I led the rest of our crew toward
the first of the two caves. I *sooked* hedgehog holes and
wild dog scat up to the entryway, where Dad unclipped
my leash.

"Find em!"

I rushed in to explore the lobby, sniffing odors of rot
and mold. My eyes adjusted to the darkness, and I
could see rooms flanking a long hallway that dropped
deep into the earth. I followed a wall down as the
space turned black, searching for human smells. My
only find was a goat corpse in one room that smelled
like paste.

The pack's flashlights lit up the walls behind me, and
the goat's smiling skull came into view. I ran out to let
Dad know that our opponents were gone. Dad gave
me a *sook* and I scanned the cave again to confirm there
were no bombs, bumping into some of my stealthy
packmates. I returned to Dad's odor and followed his
voice out to the light.

At the exit, a metal spoon on the wall caught Dad's attention. I laid down to nibble my sore wrist while the rest of the pack checked out a piece of fishing line hanging from the spoon – it was an "unarmed trip wire" according to the pack's buzz.

We moved back outside, into the wind, and trotted across the rocky ridgeline – Dad told me to run ahead on the long leash to *sook*. The pack was on alert, and before we reached the second cave, Dad stopped and reeled me back. He gave me a few chews of a tennis ball – then he said "*los*" and put it back in his pocket, unhooking my leash. He looked me in the eyes with intense focus and sent me towards the cave with a "*sook.*"

I sniffed a lightly worn path towards the mouth of the second cavern as gusts of wind sprayed dirt in my face. I caught a bitter scent, and followed my nose to the right side of the entrance – odor was falling from a location just above me, out of reach. I sat firmly on the ground.

Dad yelled, "*here!*" and threw me the tennis ball; he held me close to him as our packmates crept up to investigate my find. They reviewed the ground at the cave's entrance, uncovering a thin cord running under the sand – it climbed up the right wall where it attached to the grenade I smelled. We watched our packmates carefully pick at the wire while enduring the cold wind that was embedding sand under my fur.

Once the wire was removed, Dad sent me in with a "*find em,*" and after I confirmed there were no players, Dad sent me back through for a "*sook.*" I hurried down another hallway into a deep pocket with no light, following the scent of explosives to a metal box where I sat and waited for Dad to appear. The air around me was stale, like it had been stuck in there for hundreds of years.

I heard Dad's boots thump toward me and then his voice. "*Here!* Good boy, *braffy.*"

I ran towards him, past my packmates crawling under the low ceiling to the metal box I'd found. After a thorough examination, they dragged the trunk out to the lobby and lifted the lid to find guns, rockets and other equipment. I gnawed on my tennis ball while they seized our opponents' weapons, adding them to our score.

We left the caves and drove back down to the road to continue our journey – weaving around the mountain's curves, above deep canyons – to arrive at a new village. Our caravan parked in a line; the pack hopped out and advanced to the nearest compound, bracing for the game to begin.

The terp made announcements and villagers assembled outside, their faces resigned. After I confirmed there were no players inside, Dad sent me back through to *sook,* but I found only the typical stuff – books, blankets, tea sets, and soaps – nothing worth a tennis ball.

As the pack swarmed the structures I sniffed the animal yard looking for goat berries, where I caught a note of sweet, rotten fruit. I tracked it to a well, rimmed by stones – the scent slowly ascended from somewhere deep underground. I balanced on the edge of the rocks, hanging my head into the hole to get a long drag. Mixed with the metalic scent of standing water, I detected the bitter smell of explosives and sat.

Dad called me to him and rubbed my head. "Good

boy," he said before peering down into the abyss and whispering, "shit."

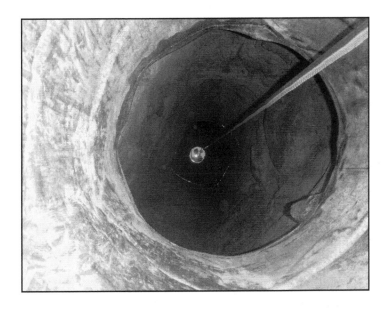

He called the pack over to investigate with flashlights, trying to determine where the bombs might be stashed. After some discussion, Dad climbed into the harness attached to a rope and pulley, and the pack lowered him down. I barked when he disappeared, demanding he resurface; I tried to jump down after him while a packmate held me back by my leash. Then I held my breath and listened to every knock and shuffle.

Finally Dad yelled, "There is a crawl space down here, and I can't see where it goes. Send Turbo down to me."

The pack attached the rope to my vest and lowered me into the darkness. I was suspended in space, my vest tight under my own weight. The only sounds were my heart pounding and the creak of the pulley.

I felt my Dad's hands pulling me into a tunnel – it was so cramped I could hardly stand up. Dad attached a glowing light to my collar and had me face into the earth, commanding me to "*sook*." I inched forward, following the curve of the passage until it dropped down into a deeper chamber. It was too dark to see into the room, but I could smell a brew of explosives inside. I sat down at the ledge, earning another ball award.

"We found something!" Dad yelled up the well. He called me back and reattached my vest to a rope that lifted me up to the pack. I was happy to feel the ground on my feet, but I immediately perched myself on the well's rim to wait for Dad. I watched as buckets full of guns, rockets, bags, and metal plates appeared from inside the well – each time disappointed by the reveal. Dad was the last to appear, and I spun in circles.

The pack stacked our opponents' equipment into a towering pile, and then decorated it with wires and white bricks like a holiday tree. We all ducked down behind a building – Dad covered my ears – and blew the mound. A wave of heat warmed our faces. Thick smoke flooded into the sky, covering the sun; an orange glow cast over the village. We walked back to the convoy as our stomachs settled, passing villagers who seemed surprisingly unfazed by the commotion; then we hopped into our warm cars and drove back to camp.

****

Dad and I awoke early one spring morning, just before daylight, and he announced to our packmates that it was my sixth birthday. I stretched my sore legs and circled the tent to receive a round of pets as he loaded up our gear; then we walked out to the waiting vehicle convoy. Our pack drove north, arriving just outside of a rundown village as the sun reached the highest point in the sky.

We exited the car and walked up a rocky path, with Dad and I leading the line. I smelled decay and urine as we reached the hilltop and adobe structures came into view below. They appeared abandoned, thatch roofs missing – the whole area had been bombed in an event many years before, and only the broken shells remained. The ground around the ruins was littered with white lumps.

As we drew closer, the lumps crystallized into goat carcasses – hundreds of them, some had rotted to bones, others clammy, more recently dead. I sniffed the first few in my path; covered with open sores and puss; they smelled rancid. There were so many I couldn't sniff them all, so I jumped over and around the bodies.

We walked to a maze of jagged walls – the pack was quiet, guns at their noses. Inside we came upon a group of people, mostly women and children, a few dads, all coated in dirt and emitting a different odor than our regular opponents. Sharp curds and organ meat hovered around them.

Our terp talked to them in hushed tones, returning to the pack to explain that these were nomads, drifting from place to place. He said they didn't have any equipment because they weren't members of our opponents' team, but Dad still had me *sook* the area anyway. As I sped around searching for bombs, the nomads floated away from me as though pushed by an invisible hand.

Unfortunately I had an opposite, almost magnetic effect on the goats, and I was quickly caught up in their mob – there were as many live ones swarming around as there were dead ones rotting on the ground. Most of the living were young, inbred, their eyes blank. They followed me around, clogging my path and babbling – *do you have milk, have you seen my mother, do you want to play?* I tried to ignore them and stay on task, but the little zombies circled me every time I paused to sniff. Irritated, I started juking them like Trainer Ben's fend-it devices.

I found no odors worthy of a tennis ball, but many interesting ones. Propped against one wall I found three fresh goat corpses, shorn naked. They were headless and legless below the elbows, just a torso with four little stubs. A long line of stitches along their bellies held in an organ and herb stuffing, and based on the bloat, they had been simmering for days under the sun. I smelled the same odors on the nomads – this was their standard fare.

I returned to Dad to give him the all clear, but the game wasn't over yet. The pack pushed past clumps of goats, over to a corral made of thorn bushes and covered with a tarp. Dad rolled a big bramble out of the entryway, releasing an ammonia plume so pungent it took several blinks to clear our eyes.

Dad pulled a handkerchief over his nose and mouth, and sent me inside with a "*sook.*" I stepped into a mush of urine-soaked hay and droppings, warm from the sun, and hopped quickly to a villager's mat lying on the ground. The scent was stifling, but I confirmed there were no bombs hidden in the sludge.

Behind the compound ruins, our pack discovered a hill carved out by intertwining tunnels. We hiked up to the one cave mouths, stepping over dead goats while being harassed by the live ones – they were sobbing, and infected with disease; blisters in their noses, drooling mouths, and poop draining down their legs. Dad pushed them away from me with his feet. We searched the tunnels, thick with stench, but the pack found no signs of games being played.

We walked back down to the village rubble, and the terp spoke briefly to the villagers before we started the long trek over the hills, back to the vehicles. We didn't get far before we ran up against a herd of goats struggling up a small incline.

I was busy *sooking* the road behind them for explosives, and I quickly closed in on the herd's stragglers. The two in the back looked over their shoulder every few seconds, whining and further holding up their own progress – then, suddenly, their legs seemed to harden. They hobbled forward a couple more steps, as if on stilts – but the rigidity spread up to their torsos and into their necks. Then they both dropped, lying in the road motionless, legs straight up in the air.

I stopped and looked back at Dad – his face was stunned. "Hey, did you see those goats drop?" he asked.

"Yeah!" one of our packmates responded. "What the hell kind of disease do they have? Now they are just keeling over?"

The pack murmured about the disease as another packmate came to the front, looking down at the frozen goats. "Nahh, their not dead," he said calmly. "They're fainting goats. We have them back in Pennsylvania. They'll get back up, watch."

I knew they weren't dead – they didn't have the smell of sweet gas; their hearts were still pumping blood through their bodies. Dad called me back with a nervous "*here*," and I ran back to him. The goats woke up – they shook off the trance and rolled themselves upright, prancing to rejoin their herd.

I ran forward, trying to capsize them again, but Dad pulled me back on the leash. The herd finally veered off the road, and I finished *sooking* the path to the vehicles. We loaded up and drove back the same way we'd come, passing the caves and stopping along the way to search for bombs.

When we neared Sadeek Village, the cars rolled off the road to park so we could visit our friends. The men and women greeted Dad "the Dog Angel" and their faces smiled as I roamed the village within my leash range. I ignored the busy moms and sniffed a couple of kids poking sticks into the dirt. The elders had a meeting with the pack that involved a lot of pointing and nodding.

I followed one of our packmates into the adjacent

animal pen, and watched him strike up a conversation with a tall donkey, about twice my size.

"Hi Mr. Donkey – you mind if I take a piss here?" he asked.

The donkey did mind – not so much about the piss as the noise. The donkey's ears rotated backwards and he began reversing towards the back of the compound; but my packmate followed him into the corner.

"Where you going? Hey, I'm talking to you, donkey."

The pack snickered, and shouted warnings.

"Dude, that donkey looks like he's getting pissed. You better leave him alone!"

"Yeah man, you show that donkey who's the bigger ass!"

I could tell the donkey was getting nervous, and I wanted to see if I could make him fall over like the goats, so I stalked up behind him – he looked back at me out of the corner of his eye, taking a few steps away and looking for a way out. I hustled forward, pressing him to faint; but he got angry instead, and bolted toward my packmate – his front legs rose high in the air and came down with a thud.

The stomp didn't startle me, but the roar from my

packmate did – the donkey's hoof had slammed down on his foot, and he was furious. The donkey and I both ran off in separate directions.

The pack laughed at our mate as he hopped around on one leg in agony; Dad examined his foot and determined that it wasn't broken inside. We helped our friend into a truck and drove back to camp, conceding that fight to the donkey.

****

Dad began stuffing our game gear into metal travel boxes, and one morning, he sheared the red fuzz off his face. I hadn't seen his chin in a long time, and neither had the sun. He began to relax more, lying in his rack with his morning coffee and singing when the tent's music came on. Our time in Afghanistan was coming to an end, and we were celebrating.

The rest of our pack was also bundling up their game gear, but Dad and I were the first to leave. We said goodbye to our pack – some of the best players and pile builders in the business.

When the helicopter flew in, Dad loaded our boxes and bags into its rear. I was ready and excited to start the journey home – but when Dad gave me a "*hoog*" to jump onto the helicopter, my front legs made it onto the deck, but my back legs didn't have enough spring. I tried to pull myself up, but I melted down the side and fell back to the ground.

"You okay boy? You okay *braffy*?" Dad asked, rushing up to help.

I looked up at him. I had been hiding pain in my hips and joints for weeks to avoid that expression. He walked over and lifted me into the helicopter, and I lay down amongst the rest of our gear as he finished loading it inside. Dad hopped on board and examined my hindquarters, massaging my knees and hamstrings as we lifted off the ground.

Chapter **8**

Coming Home

The helicopter landed at the camp we stayed in during our first deployment tournament – I could smell the poop ponds before we got off the bird. We visited our old room and then walked back out to the tarmac where we boarded a C-17. I spent most of the long flight in my kennel, with a few breaks to unfold my aching legs and sniff the other passengers, strapped into seats along the plane's sides. We lived in a hotel for one night – sharing the room's bed until Dad's twitching sent me to the floor – in a town near the ocean that smelled like fresh bread.

The next plane landed in America, and we ran down the back ramp onto a familiar tarmac under a misty night sky. I stretched my legs and took a long pee in the grass, breathing in clean, dewy air. Dad gave me a cup of water and a handful of food, and we boarded another plane.

"You ready to go home and see mom? Take a nap on the couch?" he asked. My head tilted at the excitement in his voice.

A few hours later we landed again – the door opened to the harsh light of a cloudy morning. Our bodies creaked as we stumbled down the ramp on stiff legs. As our feet touched solid ground, we saw a group of humans dressed in game gear, walking towards us with purpose. Dad talked to them while I sniffed the hardscape, finding a few empty seashells and old cigarette butts that smelled like mouths. I stopped – my ears perked – when I heard Dad's voice get loud.

"You have got to be fucking kidding me!" he yelled; but whatever they said, he didn't think it was funny. I sprinted over to him, sitting at his left side – ready for action.

"The rules state that he has to stay in a kennel facility," one of the men said. "He can't go with you."

I saw pain in Dad's face – his brow furrowed, his eyes searching for answers – as he realized he had no choice. These were the rules, they repeated.

He told a man to hold my leash and barked at them to "wait a minute," as he collected my kennel, bedding, and empty water bowl and placed them next to me. Then he piled his game gear in front of a waiting van.

My tail wagged when he started walking back. He leaned down and put his hands on my face, and we touched our foreheads together.

"Okay, buddy, you have to go with these guys. You can't come with me," he said, his voice cracking. " I'm so sorry," he whimpered. His eyes were tired and wet.

I still wasn't expecting Dad to leave without taking my leash from the stranger's hand, but he turned and walked away, getting inside of the van without me. I ran to be with him, but the leash held me back, and I watched the van door slide closed. Then the stranger with my leash started marching towards a gray building, dragging me along behind him. I spun in quick circles to watch the van depart, vanishing into the fog.

He tugged me into a concrete facility that smelled like piss, and led me into a cell. My travel crate, floor mat and bowl were rolled down the hall to their own cage. I lapped water from a bowl fixed to my cage front, and a few minutes later a guard came by and poured a scoop of kibble into a second attached bowl.

"So your name is Turbo, huh?"

I looked up at the sound of my name to scan his face, but he turned and walked away, down the corridor. As he passed the other dogs he triggered waves of desperate barks, but didn't seem to notice.

After several hours in solitary I was still hungry and in need of a recess. I tried to sleep, but as the daylight disappeared, I finally gave in and shit in the corner of my cage – I couldn't hold it any longer. After several more hours, I also relieved my bladder.

Hours passed. At some point a guard appeared with a hose to spray my waste into a concrete ditch that ran behind the cells. The rush of water drenched everything in the cage, including me, and I was left standing in a dirty puddle. The guard appeared again later to fill my bowl with kibble. I ate and curled up in the driest corner of the cage, shivering as the cool night drafts swept over my wet fur.

The next day was warm, and many of my neighbors had sick stomachs; their waste hung in the air. I split my time between long naps and pacing, looking for an exit. I was obsessed with Dad, my ears perking at every sound, wondering when he would come rescue me... but as daylight came and went, over and over again, with more feedings and spray downs by a guard who rarely looked at me, I started to wonder whether I would ever see him again.

It was a late afternoon when I heard the pounding of boots, echoing across the cement floors. I knew before I smelled the first hint of peppermint that it was Dad, and my tail went crazy. I saw his figure round the corner – he was commanding the guard to pull my crate out from storage. He ran when he saw me, and both of us let out a few excited yelps as he worked the cage latch. The door popped open and I leapt and squealed – but Dad quickly attached my leash and whispered, "Let's get out of here."

We trotted past the other inmates as they called after us, "*Take me with you!*" We ran out to the parking lot, where Dad gave me a "*hoog*" into the truck; the doors slammed shut, and we sped away from the prison. I danced – free again and back with Dad. Everything was right with the world.

We drove to a hotel near the airfield. Dad lugged our bags into the room, and I jumped onto the plush white bed, rolling onto my back to give my legs a good stretch. I fought to keep my eyes open – not let Dad out of my sight – but that was a battle I quickly lost.

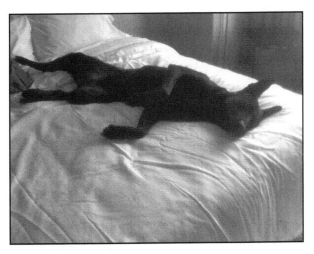

After my first real nap in days, Dad woke me up to

walk over to a park, full of velvety grass as far as I could see. I sprinted after a ball, ignoring the pain in my hips. We spent two nights in the hotel – still uneasy, our sleep interrupted by muffled barks – before we packed up our gear and boarded a plane for home.

We jostled and rolled to a hard stop in San Diego, and the plane doors opened to let in the balmy night air. Dad and I hopped out, pulling bags and gear behind us when we saw Mom's arms waving at the end of the tarmac. She rushed over to claim Dad, holding his face in her hands as they hummed into each other's ears. Then she leaned down and hugged me tight.

"Thank you for bringing him home safe," she whispered. "I missed you both so much!"

She continued to cuddle me while Dad loaded our gear in the car. Then we drove towards my two favorite places in the world – the park and home.

****

Back in San Diego, things had changed since I left
– Loki and Hammer had retired; Jazz had just left
for deployment, and Speedy had not yet returned. I
entered the kennel house to find new dog odors.

I barked hello to Diesel and puppy Ace, and introduced
myself to our new pack members. Dexter was a tall
Dutchie with jaws like an alligator – he could jump
all the way to the top of a lamppost to sniff out a
scent. Our other rookie, Nitro, was a young Belgian
with sharp teeth and angular black eyes. Feisty like a
badger, he was a handful for the dads.

Speedy arrived home a few days later. I greeted my old
pal with a bark and a tail wag, but he barely recognized
me – his eyes were dark and empty. Mick put him in
a kennel, where he jumped around manically, crying
out as though he was in pain. But when the dads tried
to put his collar on and give him some food, he went
ballistic, threatening to bite anything near him. His
brain was infested with spiders.

On Speedy's first night home, Mick had to leave him
alone just like Dad had left me. Sleeping in a kennel
two doors down, I listened to Speedy moan and chisel
at the metal door with his teeth. I tried to ignore it, but
all night long he worked on the wires of his cage – a
shrill, clinking melody.

The dads arrived in the morning, and I heard a lot of "holy shits" as they discovered Speedy's work. He had opened up a thorny hole in his kennel door, mangling his mouth in the process. His head was covered in blood from gashes in his gums and forehead, where he had scraped himself trying to squeeze through the passage. They examined his mouth – several of the teeth were ground down to nubs. Speedy was taken away in a plastic travel crate, returning a week later with a shiny new set of metal fangs.

A few weeks after coming home, I rejoined Trainer Ben's classes – I was an expert at all of the events, but my legs were letting me down. During my first fight with Trainer Ben, I hit him hard and countered all of his tricks, forcing him to concede the fight. It was a clear victory – I ran proudly back to Dad, limping on my sore knee and holding my wrist off the ground. Dad kneeled at my side to rub my legs, then he lifted me into the car and we ended our training day early. I sat at the window and watched the newbies perform – their technique was sloppy, but their bodies were elastic.

Dad and I spent the next day sitting in an office cubicle. I sniffed the filthy wool carpet while he barked into a telephone, yelling about "injuries," "wear and tear," and "two combat deployments." The voices on the other end were monotone, which got Dad even more riled up. Eventually I lay down and slipped into a dream –

chasing the people behind the telephone voices, biting and shaking them while Dad cheered, "*Yah, braffy! That's my boy!*"

****

Dad and I stopped attending practice; we spent our days confined to his office and our nights at home, where I got to sleep on the couch.

I was living at home on the 4th of July when family and friends came to visit us, arriving with armfuls of food. I slipped around under friendly hands looking for snacks while our guests ate and listened to music. Later that night they crowded onto the back patio, and suddenly the sky exploded with blasts of light and noise. I panicked – *the game had come to San Diego.* I looked at Dad, who also seemed uncomfortable.

"It's okay, Turbo. They're just fireworks," Dad said as I scanned the house for opponents, my ears folded down reflexively with the whistles and booms. He took me over to the couch, and told me to "*hoog.*"

"I don't like them either," he said. "Don't worry, *braffy,* you *bliven.* It will be over soon – I promise." He put his hands over my ears.

We returned to work a few days later to run a competition course that started with a long *sook* event. I located the smells without trouble, but limped through the long trek and took a few extra recesses. I faltered down a mountainous crevasse, teetering on the uneven ground as I tried to dart around to find the odors. Trainer Ben said I had "too much wear and tear," as he scratched marks on a clipboard. Then a huge blast detonated right behind me, and my tail and ears tucked. Dad shook his head at Trainer Ben.

Our last event was a "*find em*," and I sprinted toward Trainer Ben in his puffy suit. I slammed him and bit hard, whipping my head from side to side; but when Trainer Ben kicked my leg, I yelped. Trainer Ben conceded the fight, and I hobbled back to Dad on my throbbing wrist.

After my subpar showing, Dad and I spent the rest of our days in the office. The confinement made Dad crazy – his blood pressure rose and he barked at all the voices on the phone. I lowered my head and drifted into dreams where Dad and I were playing on the beach, and when he threw the ball into the fizzy waves, I ran after it with no pain.

Epilogue

I finally figured out why Dad had been so angry – he had been negotiating my release. When the last piece of paper was signed, I was officially adopted. Dad and I were family, bonded for life.

After three years of training and competing, Dad and I left the dog team to become BUD/S instructors. Now we teach new meats how the games are played. One of my favorite events is when Dad makes them "hit the surf." They lie in the ocean while I run around over top of them. Sometimes I hide their canteens, and the other instructors and I have a good laugh watching a student try to figure out where it is buried.

Another great thing about retirement is Mom. Of course, she was always around, joining Dad and I on weekend trips to the kennels where she cleaned cages, washed bowls, and collected poops. She can't throw the ball as hard as Dad, and she is terrible at tug, but if cuddling is a sport then she is its champion. Many of my filthy roommates over the years have signed up for her cuddling events – Diesel would lean his weight against her as she scrubbed his matted fur until her hands were black. She was one of the few people that Loki loved – their cuddlefests were never long enough for him. Back then, I was too busy searching for a tennis ball to sit and snuggle.

Now I finally understand the wonder of having a Mom. On mornings when my back legs have frozen up, she rubs them until they are limber enough to run again. And on days when Dad goes to work without me, Mom takes me to her office where my girlfriend Linda greets me at the door with a treat, and a new pack welcomes me with scratches and hugs – tons of rewards, and no games required. I curl up in a big leather chair and nap until the afternoon, when I take Mom on a walk – she lets me pick the route and pretends not to notice when I snack on bunny raisins along the way.

On Saturdays, Mom and I watch the birds. She fills their wooden houses with seeds, and they flock to the area to argue and feast. Sometimes I charge out and scatter them, to remind them that they are free.

At night, Mom kisses my nose way too many times, whispering "Goodnight, sweet boy." And she doesn't ask for anything in return – who knew such humans existed?

Best of all, she likes to hear my stories...

Glossary of Dog Training Terms

Aufliggen/Auf	Lie down
Bliven	Stay
Braffy	Term of endearment
Fas (German)	Bite command
Find em	Search for opponents
Fooey	Stern "no" command
Fooligan	Follow the handler in a left heel
Gib-lout	Speak/bark
Hoog	Jump over or onto something
Los	Let go/Release (of a ball/bite)
Plotz (German)	Lie down
Platz (Dutch)	Sit down to handler's left
Sook/Zook	Search for object/scent
Stellan (Dutch)	Bite command
Zit	Sit

About the Author

R.C. Cook is the proud Mom of Senior Chief Turbo. This is her first novel, and a labor of love.

Acknowledgments

Great love and appreciation goes out to the "dads" and dogs that have inspired the characters. And thanks to Speedy's dad for naming him.

To all of our packmates – thank you for the stories and the friendship.

Thanks to family and friends for reading the manuscript – particular thanks to David for helping me find the voice.

Finally, a very special thanks to David Fairrington for his vision and passion – it is a great honor to feature his art on the cover.

Made in the USA
San Bernardino, CA
04 December 2014